MOONDANCE

MOONDANCE

STEPHEN LAWRENCE

authorHOUSE®

AuthorHouse™
1663 Liberty Drive
Bloomington, IN 47403
www.authorhouse.com
Phone: 1-800-839-8640

The story, its characters and events that are contained in this book are all fictitious. Although names and places may be familiar to friends and family, the content is written purely from my own imagination. Anyone mentioned is in no way connected to, or associated with anything that is; unlawful, an organization, or committee that intends to commit unlawful acts or events.

Factual mistakes or misrepresentation are solely the fault of the author.

My website. www.stephenlawrencebooks.com

Published by AuthorHouse   11/16/2012

ISBN: 978-1-4772-4666-5 (sc)
ISBN: 978-1-4772-4667-2 (e)

ACKNOWLEDGEMENTS.

I would like to thank my family and friends,
for their encouragement and involvement
in helping me to write this story.

Special thanks to Chris Fitzpatrick "Chrissy"
for her help on this novel.

FOREWORD.

Detective Chief Inspector Derek Williams and his team at Gloucestershire CID, have been trying to track down a serial killer terrorizing Cheltenham Town for several months. They know it is only a matter of time before the killer, who they believe is a woman, will strike again, but they don't know where, when or who.

Will they be able to stop her before she claims another innocent victim?

During their investigations they stumble across some other dirty dealings, tax evasion and drug running. The police combine forces to take them down, but will it all go to plan?

ONE.

Brian Fielding was walking home after a night at the pub with his mates. He had just devoured a steak & kidney pie and large portion of chips, eating it out of the chip shop wrapping paper while he was walking along. This was his usual routine on a Friday night.

As he tossed the empty wrapping papers into a waste bin on the side of the pathway, he thought he might just take a quick detour through the park.

The reason being was that Brian was single, and not very attractive to women, so he often rounded off his regular Friday night out at the pub, by paying for sex with a hooker, who were usually found loitering in the region of the local parks.

Tonight the moon was bright, so even though most of the pathway lights that encircled the park had been vandalized, it was easy for Brian to see a good way ahead.

He was nearing the middle of the park before she stepped out from behind the shadows of the bushes that lined part of the walk. She was quite tall in her high heels, she wasn't one that he had used before, so he was looking her up and down, feeling excited at the thought of having sex with a new girl.

As he stepped up to her, he could see the smile on her face, the bright red lipstick, the long blonde hair, the short fur coat above the very short skirt and the fishnet stockings on her long legs.

He started to ask how much it was going to cost him . . . . but all he managed to say was

'Hey babe, how mu . . . . aghh!'

At that moment all he saw was a glint of something shiny flash across his midriff, and then he was sinking to his knees. His intestines and inners were spilling out of his white shirt, just as though someone had opened a zip fastener to allow the contents to be ejected.

As he crumpled to the ground, kneeling in the pool of blood and offal that was quickly leaving his body, his hands as if automatic, clutched at the gaping wound above the belt on his jeans.

He managed to raise his head to look at his attacker as she stood over him, looking down and smiling at him, seemingly pleased with her work. She was smiling while humming a tune he thought he recognized, as she calmly pushed him backwards with the sole of her foot against his shoulder so that he was laid out flat on his back.

Strangely enough he was in no pain now, but felt as though he were in the middle of a dream. Everything seemed to be in slow motion. Surreal.

Before the blackness came, he remembered the title of the song.

As he lay there the pool of blood, she very carefully removed his watch, rings and wallet from his person. Careful not to step in the blood or leave any clue that could be followed.

Carol was dressed as someone would expect a prostitute to resemble, but her intention was not to have sex, only to kill her prey quickly and efficiently and then take whatever valuables and money they possessed. Anything accept mobile phones. She didn't want to risk any chance of being plotted by GPS, or whatever clever technological systems the authorities could use to track people. Though tempted sometimes, because some of her victims had top of the range phones which she could probably get a lot of money for, she always left them behind whatever make or model.

It was another part of her MO. Revenge was her motive from the beginning, but now she was beginning to enjoy it and the takings was her extra pocket money, for the little luxuries she couldn't generally afford.

She didn't need drugs, killing scum was how she got on a high, and Brian Fielding was her fifth victim and just another piece of shit on her shoe that she had just scraped off.

Now she was like an expert when she slashed her prey across the midriff, and as they lay in their own bloody inners, she would, as a last precaution, make sure with a final slice through the carotid artery on the neck of her chosen victim.

Tonight had felt good, as it was at least six weeks since her last "night out". But the time between kills was getting shorter, as her greed and thirst for revenge was becoming more addictive.

She quickly checked around the crime scene to make sure it was a clean kill and that she had left no trace of her identity. Only the neatness of her work, the same cuts, the same M.O the police called it.

Yes, her *Modus Operandi* would identify her as the same killer as that of the others.

She was happy with her work, and strode off briskly humming *that tune!* Then disappearing into the moonlit evening, back to her bolt hole where she would examine her rewards, and remember the thrill of the evenings work over a few shots of vodka.

Fifteen minutes later and she was at the back entrance of her hidey hole apartment.

She parked her car on the wasteland at the end of the road. It was dark up there and she could walk up the back road to the houses without being noticed. Up the fire escape stairs and within another minute she was inside the dingy living space which was situated above a launderette.

She rented the whole upper floor, which had a front access door from the main street via stairs next to the front entrance of the launderette and a rear access via the fire escape, which was perfect for her little escapades. The dwelling allowed her to enter at the front as one person, and out through the back as another. Anyone watching would only see an inconspicuous person entering the front of the building, a very different person to the one that used the back stairway.

The property was set in the middle of a row of tiny terraced houses that were converted to shops on the ground floor, and lodgings above. In the row of six, the one end was a fish and chip shop, then an off licence, the launderette, a kiddies clothes shop, a charity odds and sods shop and at the other end a corner shop which sold just about anything. Other than that the road was rows of small terraced houses, split by the odd pair of semi-detached to break them up a bit. The fire escape at the rear came down into a square of concrete about ten feet square, the rear garden, with a gate into a dark back alleyway.

Beyond the alley was a field, and the property was owned by a cardboard making factory which was at least a hundred yards from the fencing that lined the alleyway. Not all the properties had fire escape stairs at the back, which probably broke the fire regulations. There was a door into the back of the launderette, but it was blocked by eight empty pallets and bags of rubble so nobody could get in or out of there.

She rented the room from the owner of the launderette, he was foreign and spoke very little English, she thought he was probably Greek or of some similar descendance. All the better to hide her identity from the authorities should they ever enquire. He would surely confuse anyone who might come snooping around, with his undecipherable dialect, and would almost certainly not be letting on to the authorities that he rented out the upper floor.

The space she rented, consisted of a bathroom with a tiny bath which had a shower head attached; a badly soiled toilet and a cracked washbasin with a small mirrored cabinet above it, also complete with a crack across the middle.

The living room was in an L shape, where she had one cushioned chair, a small coffee table and a drawer unit against the wall. It had a large window with grubby net curtains, which looked out onto the main road. The small kitchenette at the opposite end had a window which overlooked the alleyway, with faded yellow curtains hanging on nails over the grubby nets covering the view to the back of the house. In there she had a small kitchen table with one chair. The fire escape exit door was in the corner. Her little bedroom consisted of a single bed against the side wall and chest of drawers on the opposite wall, and a chair. This room also had a window overlooking the street, complete with the grubby net curtains.

The stairs from the front entrance came up into the corner of the living room. All the walls were wallpapered which was ripped and scraped in places, and the damp in the corners of the rooms was turning the yellow paper into moldy black. The floors had a covering of linoleum which had also seen better days.

The state of the apartment did not matter, because all she needed was a place to change, shower and hide her "takings" after the event. She often left valuables like watches, jewellery and credit cards there, not hidden, but simply left in the chest of drawers until she could return maybe a few days later to take them to Birmingham.

She had a contact up there, who would exchange them for cash and then sell the goods on.

She undressed and put all her clothes and the latex gloves she wore, into a black bin bag. When she returned in a day or two, she would wash the clothes at the launderette downstairs, or, if they were too badly stained she would burn them along with the gloves in the old oil drum in the back yard.

After taking a shower, she wrapped in a bath towel, then poured herself a drink, lit a cigarette and sat in her solitary chair while she perused her trophies. She had a watch, two rings, one gold neck chain, and a brown leather wallet. The wallet contained eighty five pounds, two credit cards, an old cinema ticket, a receipt for some shopping items from Morrison's, a driver's license and a photo of two little girls.

She wondered if they could be his daughters. She felt a moment of guilt. There was no photo of a wife or partner. Maybe he was divorced or a single parent. *'Why should I give a fuck anyway!'* she thought. *'The pervert got what he had coming to him.'*

She could see from the license that the victim's name was Brian Fielding and was aged about thirty seven.

After getting dressed and one or two more shots of vodka, she left as the person she entered as, out of the front entrance.

It was only a short walk to the end of the road to the car, and back to her normal life . . . until next time.

TWO.

Dave, Kev, Spike and Craig, who had been best mates for a number of years, were sat in their local, "The Empty Jug" having a regular Saturday afternoon pint and game of cards.

Danny the landlord, was at the bar reading the early edition of "The Cheltenham Echo" the local newspaper. On the front page was a report of another killing, who the police believed to be the **"Fifth victim of a serial killer on the loose in Cheltenham"**.

The lads all looked up as they heard Danny say, *'Shit!'* out loud.

'Hey, Dan the man, we don't allow language like that in here.' Spike said jokingly.

The others smiled at Spike's usual nature of playing the cheeky chap. He was always looking for a laugh, or to play one of his pranks on an unsuspecting punter.

Dan didn't look up, he just carried on reading what details the newspaper had printed about the latest murder victim.

Craig got up to get another round in at the bar. He looked at the story that Danny was reading, and even though it was upside down, he could read the headline. **"Victim number five"**. He guessed that the mysterious serial killer had struck again somewhere in the region of the town.

'Fucking hell Dan, you can't even go for a night out around here anymore, without the chance of getting your gut slashed open can you?' Said Craig.

'Well, you won't find me strolling through any park late at night with that crazy bitch on the streets.' He replied.

'How do you know it's a woman?'

'Police have said that it's more than likely some old pro gone a bit nutty, who likes to just take the money and not give any nooky in return.' Said Danny.

'Is that really what the cops are saying there?' Craig asked pointing at the column in the newspaper.

'Well not exactly, but it states that they haven't ruled out the possibility that a woman could be the killer, but that's who they suspect isn't it, because all the killings have been in areas where the pro`s are . . . but they say there is no sign that the victim had had sex before he got done over . . . poor bastard never even got a last blowjob before he copped it; Anyway . . . what're you lads up to tonight then?' Danny asked as he ditched the paper and started to pull the four pints.

'Were off to the town hall . . . 60's night, you know, old bands and that from your era' said Spike.

'Cheeky bastard . . . them were the good old days, proper music, better than this rap and house music shit they're playing these days anyway.'

'You're right there Dan,' said Kev. 'We all enjoy the old stuff, he's just pulling your pisser.'

'Anyway, Spike has to do what his misses says' Dave joined in, 'or he won't get his wicked way with her when he gets home tonight.'

'Fuck off you lot, I do what I want, when I want' Spike said.

Danny came back with . . . 'Well just don't get chasing them old tarts in the park, or you might get your nuts cut off . . .'

'No chance of that tonight mate' said Kev. 'The women are coming with us.'

They played cards and the drink flowed till it was around six, then Craig got up first to go.

'Right then lads, I'm off to have some grub and take a shower before we go out tonight, see you outside the hall at what, seven thirty?'

'Yep that should be early enough for us to get in and down the front by the stage' said Dave.

They were all gone within minutes of each other, leaving Danny still browsing through his papers at the bar, and no more than half a dozen other people having a casual drink after their Saturday shopping sprees.

Danny and his wife Maggie had been the pub owners and landlords of "The Empty Jug" in Leckhampton— Cheltenham—Gloucestershire for about six years now, and had a good reputation with the local punters.

The bar was one large single bar room divided into three sections; the main bar area at the front with a large window looking out onto the main street, the snug in the middle section with trellis to the ceiling to partition it off, then there was a games section at the back which had a pool table, dart board and a shoveha'penny slate.

Dan and Maggie were easy going people, both in their mid fifties and enjoying the time behind the bar themselves. They only employed two extra bar staff on Friday and Saturday nights to cope with the crowds who came out of the local restaurants, curry houses and cinema that were along the same road.

Each year they endeavored to have at least two holidays abroad, the first was usually a couple of weeks in Malta where they owned a holiday apartment, that would be around February time. The second break would usually be a cruise somewhere later on in the year, so that they could sit back and enjoy being waited on for a couple of weeks before returning to run the pub again. When they went on holiday, a stand-in landlord was brought in.

Craig was home within ten minutes, he only lived just around the corner from the pub at his parent's house on the Leckhampton estate.

His mother is the full time carer for his dad, who suffers with Alzheimer's. Craig is an insurance salesman, a job he took reluctantly two and a half years ago because there was no other work around the area at that time. His wages are mostly on bonuses from selling life policies, so he spends many an evening in some stranger's house trying to talk them into buying large insurance policies.

He is engaged to Sarah Hepworth, and they have been together now for nearly three years, shortly after the time that Craig and his parents had moved to Cheltenham. They met at the Town Hall bar during the interval when they both went there to see Chubby Brown in concert.

She works in the fashion department as a window dresser, in a large department store in town, and is also living at home with her mum and dad, who have a nice house in the Charlton Kings area. Craig has been getting a lot of earache from her lately about them living apart with parents, but they just can't seem to get enough money together for a deposit to put down on their own place, and she isn't at all happy about that. She feels that she is doing all she can to build their joint account, but Craig always gives the excuse of not earning enough money or bonuses, to be able to spare money for their house fund.

She doesn't like him going to the pub so often, because the money he spends on beer and card gambling could be saved towards their own home. Well that's how she sees it anyway.

But Craig is in no hurry for them to move in together, although he really loves Sarah, he's not too keen on giving up his freedom, his nights out with the boys and his Saturday afternoon beer, ciggy`s and card games.

They have a good social life that Craig enjoys, his fear is losing that if they have their own house, because Sarah would tighten the purse strings. So for now he's quite content to carry on living at home and seeing Sarah as and when he likes.

Sex was difficult for them sometimes because of the lack of privacy, but they managed when the parents were out or just made out in the car. Sarah said it made her feel cheap, like a slapper, and she often refused to do it in protest. She said that if they had their own home, they would have the freedom to have sex in private and without any restrictions. Craig saw it more as a turn on, and rather liked the thought of getting caught in the act.

Tonight they were on their way out to the town hall with Dave & Karen, Kev & Lynn, and Spike with his current girlfriend.

Spike, real name Steve Williams, so called because of his spiky hair cut, wasn't as steady as the others, in that he usually had a girlfriend for a few months, then got fed up and would go solo for a while, until someone else came along.

His trade is in heating, ventilation and general plumbing. He has his own business, and is doing well for himself, there's plenty of work coming in and he's earning good money for it, so he recently took on a young lad as an apprentice, and also a couple of other casual workers onto his books.

He owns an apartment in Tivoli mews, quite a posh area on the edge of town, all bought and paid for, no mortgage. His car is a top of the range BMW which of course he has as an aid to his favorite hobby, women.

Any woman who looked his way would get that irresistible smile and the chat up lines from him, and he was very good at that. He generally picked up his women when he went out to quote for work. Women came and went with him regularly, and the lads agreed that he would probably be middle aged before he settled down, but for now he was having a great time.

His current conquest was Angie, a very pretty beauty technician who owns her own business in the town centre, and after providing a successful quote, he had the job of fitting a new hot water system in her shop. He fitted the system personally because he knew he would score with her.

Although Spike is very well off, he's never bragged about his wealth, he likes to brag about the women but never money. The crew he is going out with tonight are his best mates, and he would do anything for them and anybody else he knew. He was known to be the "cheeky chappie" of the bunch.

Kev, another of the Saturday quartet and Lynn his wife, have been married for two years, and are as steady as a rock. Both of them made for each other and both so easy going. They have just moved into their own house in Pittville near the park, after living in a rented flat since they got married. Kev works as a mechanic in a local garage, and in his spare time his passion is kickboxing, in which he's a third Dan black belt. He also helps to run the kickboxing school with another black belt. He makes a little money from that after the expenses of paying for the hall are taken out, but he doesn't do it for the money anyway, he purely loves the sport.

Lynn works in the same department store as Sarah, only she works on the perfume and makeup counter. She's a Yoga and keep fit fanatic, so she and Kev are well suited for each other. They both have their own things to do in the week, but the weekend is time out with the usual gang. Like Spike, they don't have money worries, both are in steady work and neither smoke or have any other expensive habits. But they know how to party at weekends.

Then there's Dave and Karen, the last of the troupe. They're not married or engaged but are living together in a rented 1 bed terraced house in Whaddon, on the edge of a counsel estate where there are lots of kids around, so obviously gangs of them regularly cause trouble.

Dave and Karen are a fairly quiet couple compared to the others of the group, and it takes a few drinks for them to loosen up when in company. Dave works as a contracts manager for an International haulage company, it's a good job which he enjoys, but the wages are shit for the responsible position. So, he has a little business deal going on the side with one of the drivers who also works for the company.

Because the company deals with the import of farm machinery and spares, drivers' are travelling in and out of Europe on a weekly basis, so it's easy for Dave's driver mate to bring back a stash of cigarettes and tobacco, then he and Dave have a share out, sell them off and split the takings. He's always made good money from it, and always made sure he kept Dan the landlord well stocked, so between them they've had quite a profitable racket going on. Occasionally, Craig and Spike would "buy in" and share the profits.

Other than going to the pub and keeping his music collection up together, Dave has no other interests in much of anything else. Fags, beer and music that's him.

His wife Karen is probably the quietest of the bunch, and wouldn't say boo to a goose. She's a very slightly built girl, so perhaps it's to do with her size. She's a solicitors secretary, again a good job but the money isn't there yet. She still has to finish her exams to qualify as a legal executive; another seven months and she'll complete it and hopefully get a major raise.

She's already planning how long it would be before they can move away from the little rented box they live in, to something with a nice kitchen and a dining room to entertain their friends. That's her dream.

She enjoys the social scene they have, but her main agenda is studying each evening to gain her qualification, because she couldn't bear the thought of failing the exam, it would destroy all her plans. No, failure is not an option to Karen.

THREE.

Cheltenham Town hall was built in 1902-03, in order to provide a venue for the many balls and concerts which made up the towns social calendar at the turn of the twentieth century. Until the year 1900, that role had been filled by the Old Assembly Rooms in the High Street, and it was their demolition to make way for a bank, that prompted the council to build a new and much larger hall on a new site.

The site chosen was a former bowling green, a part of Imperial Square, which at that time contained not only gardens but the large glass and steel Winter Gardens building, which has since been demolished. The designs for the building, which was built of freestone in a Baroque style, were provided by a Gloucester architect by the name of Frederick William Waller.

The town hall was rapidly built, and on December 5th 1903 was officially opened by Sir Michael Hicks-Beach MP, a former Chancellor of the Exchequer, and a man whose family had long-standing connections with Cheltenham.

The centerpiece of the Town Hall is its main hall, distinguished by its Corinthian style columns and coved ceiling. In all, including balcony seating, it holds up to 1000 people, twice the number possible in the Old Assembly Rooms. Its sprung floor is particularly suitable for dances.

The Town Hall is now used for concerts, banquets, meetings, dances, balls, exhibitions, conferences and as one of the major homes of Cheltenham Festivals.

7:30 pm.

Dave and Karen were already there, waiting outside. Spike, Angie, Kev and Lynn arrived minutes later by taxi just as Craig and Sarah were walking across from the car park opposite. They all greeted each other and made their way toward one of the queues to get in, and after ten minutes they were at the bar ordering a quick one before the first band struck up.

There was a good crowd of people in there of mixed ages, from teenagers to "fifty plus" year olds spread about in the hall. Tonight, sixties band "The Kinks" were playing, backed up by a couple of good local bands playing tribute to the "Sixties" music.

The music kicked off at nine, with one of the local bands playing a mix of sounds from Merseyside. Everyone was moving in time with the music, the whole crowd seemed to be as one as they bounced up and down on the springy floor of the hall.

After an hour the lads left the girls dancing around their handbags, like they did in the sixties, and went off to the bar for more beer. Dave, Spike and Kev stood aside while Craig got a round in, the people waiting at the bar were four deep, so it took a while.

They eventually got their beers, then they stood back from the bar, chatting and generally having a laugh. Spike was on form as usual telling a joke a minute, but then there was a sudden change in his mood and he seemed to shrink into the corner where they were standing. He had turned as white as a sheet.

'What's up mate? You look like you've seen a ghost' Craig said.

Spike didn't say anything for a while. Then he said, 'I just saw Marlene come in at the other end of the bar.'

Marlene was Spike's last girlfriend and was a bit of a psycho, that's why he ditched her after only two months. She was a bit of a vodka drinker, sinking a whole bottle a night wasn't unusual, and then the violence would begin. Spike still had scars on his back from when she sank her talons into him the first time he shagged her, because with her, there was no romantic evenings followed by lovemaking, it was just vodka followed by lustful torrid and mostly violent sex.

Of course Spike thought it was brilliant to start with, but the novelty soon wore off when his collection of wounds started to get out of control, and of course the pain that went with it.

During one frantic sex session, he thought she was going to chew the end of his knob off, she had him in her mouth giving him oral sex when she suddenly bit hard on him, causing him excruciating pain and severe bruising. She left her teeth marks around his manhood and he couldn't get a hard on for a week after because of the pain. She used to taunt him into sex, telling him that only a real man was able to satisfy her the way she liked it. So he played along with her sex games, until he finally found the courage to tell her it was over.

It was difficult for him to split from her, because of her threats. They were in his apartment the night he told her it had to finish, she just went apeshit and started to smash the place up. Spike had to call the police in the end, and she spent the night in the cells. As the police took her from his place, she had threatened him saying that she would cut him open if she ever saw him out with another woman, and he believed that she really would do it to him.

The lads knew how mad she was, Spike had showed them his scars from his sexual escapades in the pub one evening. He had also told them how scary she was, so they knew that he had reason to be shitting himself at that moment.

They decided it was best to keep away from her, and try to enjoy the evening without any trouble. They drank up and returned to the ballroom, shielding Spike from the view of psycho Marlene, and back to where the girls were still dancing the night away.

They were the far side of the stage from the doorway to the bar, and could barely see into the bar from their position, but they took it in turns to keep an eye open in case mad Marlene came near. But it was doubtful that she would leave her position at the bar, no, she was not going to be far from the bar stool she had acquired. Spike was still looking a bit pale and feeling scared, but wanted to stay and have a good time.

By the time "The Kinks" came on stage, Marlene was pissed out of her brains and had not moved from the bar, except when she was falling off her stool, which was at least three times. They decided that she was no longer a threat to Spike, as she probably wouldn't even remember the friend she came in with. The change in Spike was as though someone had flicked a switch, and he was back to his usual funny self, and dancing around like a right Nancy.

When the final group took to the stage, the friends were all sweating and knackered from dancing around so much, so decided to make their way into the bar area for another drink before going for a curry. The guys checked out the area first for any signs of Marlene, but it appeared that she'd left. They stood in the lounge bar for a further twenty minutes, before Dave suggested that they made a move before the rush to get out, and move on to the "Indian Ocean" curry house.

They were all agreed and made their way to the exit. The women said they needed to powder their noses before they left, so they went off to the ladies room, meanwhile the guys waited outside the building.

Within a minute or so, there was some sort of commotion around the ladies toilet, which was just inside the foyer, women were screaming, and the girls, along with about fifty others, all came flying out of the main doors looking pretty scared.

Kev took hold of Lynn and asked what the problem was. She was clearly shocked at something and had a job to speak.

It was Karen who said 'there's some crazy bitch in the toilet with a knife! and apparently she's already stabbed the doorman because he asked her to leave, there's blood everywhere!'

A few minutes later the place was crawling with police, who stormed into the building like a swat team going in to free hostages.

An ambulance arrived shortly after that, and the paramedics also rushed inside.

The four couples decided not to hang around but go and have that curry, and as they started to walk away the police were dragging a woman out in handcuffs.

It was Marlene. She had blood covering the front of her blouse and jeans where she had stabbed the doorman.

'OH FUCK!' said Spike, as he cowered behind the others, 'do you see who it is?'

'Lets just get the fuck out of here guys, we don't need to be involved do we!' said Kev, as he comforted Lynn who was still in a state of shock.

As they moved away from the town hall Kev decided it best if he took Lynn home, she was in no fit state for anymore excitement that evening. Spike and Angie said they would go with them as well to share the taxi. So the four said goodnight, and walked back towards the taxi rank across from the Town Hall.

Dave, Karen, Craig and Sarah walked on to the curry house.

They sat eating their order of popadoms with mint and lime pickle. Balti Chicken, Lamb Passanda, vegetable Samosas, mushroom rice, pilau rice, pashwari nan and keema nan. The conversation ranged from a good night of music and dancing to the behavior of mad Marlene.

They had witnessed her violent temper before, when they had previously been out with Spike and her, back when they were dating. One night she had upturned a table and threatened a frightened waitress in the Italian restaurant, simply because she had touched Spike on the arm and smiled at him. She accused the waitress of being an ugly whore, and told her she would rip her throat out if she came near him again.

The waitress, poor girl, was totally distraught and ran to the kitchen in floods of tears. The eight of them were promptly told to leave and were banned from going back, the owner said he would call the police to them next time.

'Hey . . . do you think she could be the serial killer, you know, the one the police are after, the one doing these guys in?' said Dave.

'Who knows' said Craig 'she seems quite capable of it, going by tonight's performance. I guess the police will be sorting her out anyway.'

'Well at least we can sleep safe in our beds tonight, knowing she's banged up until they decide what to do with her. She must have mad cow disease or something' said Sarah.

They all laughed lightly, but at the same time thinking she probably was mad and capable of killing. To think they had all sat close to her, and now knew what she was really capable of, sent a shiver through them all.

At the police station, Marlene was in a cell and under observation because of her intoxication. She was in no state to be questioned at least until the following morning.

Detective Chief Inspector Williams and Detective Sergeant Hayes were heading the serial killer case. They had been informed of the knife attack, and because of similarities in the type of attack, that being a knife slash to the gut, had arranged to be there the following morning to check out Marlene Adams and any possible connection to the five killings.

She was very quickly ruled out as the killer, once they had checked out her whereabouts at the times of the murders. She had solid proof alibis' for each occasion, which placed her at totally different locations. She would however, still face charges for the assault on the doorman. The detectives handed the case over to the uniform division to let them take care of that one.

Ironically, the serial killer was at the Town Hall the night of Marlene's attack on the doorman, but she was not out on a killing spree that evening, she was only out to enjoy the music and company of her friends, who were totally oblivious to the company they were keeping.

FOUR.

It was three weeks since the killing of Brian Fielding, and the funeral was commencing from the street where he lived with his sister Sheila. She had made the arrangements after the police had released his body for burial.

Brian had gone to live with his sister after the death of their mother five years ago. The father had gone off years earlier with another woman when the kids were young, Brian was nine and Sheila was seven, leaving the mother to fend for the son and daughter. Luckily they lived in a council house and were able to get certain benefits to live off, otherwise they would probably have been made homeless and been moved into a homeless shelter of some sort, or even into care homes.

Now, Sheila was married to Tom and had two girls, Amy three and Debbie two. They had a big house on the Hewlett road, so when the mother died they had asked Brian if he wanted to rent a room from them. He being single and having few friends jumped at the chance and had lived with them happily ever since.

He had worked for the town's parks department since leaving school, keeping the Pittville park areas tidy, and cleaning up after the litter-louts and druggies who left their discarded waste and needles lying around.

On Monday mornings at work, he would regularly go back to the area where he had had sex with the prostitute on the previous Friday night and find the used condoms that she had discarded into the bushes. This was part of his routine and he would often smile to himself at the thought of his misbehavior.

The few friends that he did have were mainly from the pub "The Howlers Arms". He played in the darts and pool teams there, and often went to the Cheltenham race meetings with the same guys. Occasionally he went out for a meal with Sheila and Tom, and sometimes they would all go to the cinema, and other times he would go alone. Otherwise he stayed in watching TV or listening to music in his room.

He never had a girlfriend or a real best mate, so was quite a lonely sort of guy. His Friday night out at the pub followed by pie and chips and a hooker in the park, was the highlight of his week.

There was the one funeral car following the hearse from the house, and they were followed by a half dozen middle aged guys who were his friends from the pub, who took their own cars.

The service was at The Holy Apostles church near Charlton Kings, then on to the cemetery.

The mourners were few but sincere for Brian, the thirty seven year old batchelor deceased.

The small crowd gathered around the coffin as it was lowered into the ground at the burial site, were unaware of the two plain clothes police detectives who were standing there with them. There was also the one sitting in the car not twenty metres away, taking photos of all who attended.

The two at the grave side were watching the attendees for reactions or anything that seemed out of place on the sad occasion. Their reports may hold some clues in the hunt for the serial killer.

The ceremony was brief, and only tears from the sister and her husband were obvious. After prayers and goodbyes to Brian, the gathering moved away slowly towards their cars.

The detectives moved away quietly and discretely, returning to the station to add their findings to the growing pile of useless information that they already had.

The mourners returned to "The Howlers Arms" where there was a buffet and drinks provided for the small gathering of family and friends of Brian.

He would be missed by his remaining family, and the few friends that he had of this world.

FIVE.

At the Police Headquarters DCI Williams and DS Hayes were working through the evidence, along with the other 8 detectives on the case.

There was a time line chart, a victim board, showing photo's of the five victims, before and after their attacks. The bloody mess in each of the after life pictures, identically portraying the MO, the "Modus Operandi" of the killer.

Time's and dates for each respective murder. Victims' names addresses, profession, work mates, friends, relatives, hobbies etc, etc, etc. There was so much information, that it covered a whole wall at the end of the incident room, but as yet there were no suspects. Apart from the evidence presented, which showed that the murderer was possibly a woman, simply because all of the victims bar one, were known to use the prostitutes around the city.

But the way the victims were dispatched did not seem to fit with a woman. It was a gut feeling of all the team. For that reason they had to keep an open mind. The killer could be male or female.

There was no rhyme or reason for these attacks, and the frustration was beginning to tell amongst the squad. DCI Derek Williams, known as "Dicky" to his friends, was ranting, and was getting really shitty with the troops because there was no progress being shown.

'Just what the hell are you fuckers getting paid for?' he said looking around the faces in the room. 'All this stuff,' waving his arm in an arc in the general direction of the evidence wall, 'and what have we got? . . . Jack fucking shit, that's what we got.' Silence held the room for what seemed like minutes.

After several long intakes of breath, he was more controlled. 'Okay listen up guys, I know we haven't had any breakthrough yet, and this sick bastard is going to slip up sometime. But! . . . and this is a big but! Unless we can find some link, a clue, a connection somewhere on this evidence wall soon . . . sure as eggs are eggs, this motherfucker whoever it is, is going to strike again . . . and we can't let that happen!'

Det. Sgt Hayes stepped up to the front of the room. 'Ok . . . we are going to pair up, break the evidence down to workable pieces, take it all apart and then put it all back together again and hope we find something we haven't spotted before. As the guv'nor said, there must be some link or connection somewhere amongst this lot,' he was now pointing at the wall.

Walking over to a flip chart and peeling the front cover over the top, he revealed the names of each detective paired to a partner, and the section to be re-investigated was all itemised on the sheet. There were a few grunts and groans about the pairings, but generally it made sense.

Reading from the sheet:-

DC Barney Miller and DC Duncan Montgomery—check out all workplace statements and timings. Employment details.

DC Keith Butler and DC Sophie Smith—check out all family statements and living arrangements etc.

DC Sharon Simmons and DC Bernie Webb—check out victims' routines, i.e. interests and pastimes, likes and dislikes, local pubs.

DC Alan McLean and DS Tim Clark—link with SOCO and review trace evidence. Victim murder locations.

DCI Derek Williams and DS Alan Hayes—review photographic and video evidence, from scenes of crime and funeral footage. Murder time line.

'Right people,' Dicky said, 'you see your task, let's not leave any stone unturned. I want you to find out every last detail of every possible, link, reason, idea or hunch, who what why where and when. I want to know whose granny farted in church, absolutely anything. I want constant updates directly to me or Alan, understood?'

There were nods all around the room.

He paused a moment for the message to sink home. The tension, the buzz in the room was overpowering. They were wound up enough.

'Ok let's go get the bastard.'

They all moved out at once, eager again to do their job.

SIX.

Tuesday around five thirty, Craig was sitting at the bar in "The Empty Jug" sipping his beer and idly chatting to Danny, when Spike came in full of his usual self.

'Hi guys what's new?'

'Not a lot mate' Craig said. Danny just looked up, nodded and proceeded to pour Spike a beer.

'Christ you're a happy bunch aren't you, what's up, you lose money on the horses or something?'

'Nah' Craig said, 'just a bit pissed off. Me and Sarah had another big barney last night, and I told her to fuck off and find another mug who wants to be tied down to a whining bitch.'

'I bet she didn't take it as a compliment then?' said Spike.

'No, not exactly' said Craig.

As Danny put Spikes' beer on the bar he says, 'Here's what you do . . . you get yourself down to the florist on the corner, buy a nice bunch of red roses, a box of Cadbury's Roses chocolates from the mini mart. Then you go round to her house tell her what a prick you are, tell her you love her and then take her out to dinner somewhere special that she likes . . . then give her a good seeing to on the backseat of the car to finish off. It always works for me!'

Spike almost choked and spluttered a mouthful of beer across the bar as he and Craig laughed at Danny's advice.

'It always works!' Danny said again, looking hurt by their mockery.

Spike then proceeded to tell Danny how it should be done. 'Danny you old fart . . . roses and chocolates went out on the ark. These days you buy them jewellery and take them to the theatre, followed by a shag on the bonnet of the car, now that's style, especially if the bonnet of the engine is warm.'

Craig seemed to cheer up a bit after listening to the guidance from two of his closest friends.

'Only one problem remaining!' He said. 'I have an appointment tonight at seven in Tewkesbury, and probably won't get back until late, so that fucks up your ideas of a perfect evening doesn't it?'

'Chuck the fucking appointment in the bin and do the right thing!' said Danny.

'He's right' said Spike, 'change the appointment to another night or something. Come on mate, you and Sarah are made for each other. You love her don't you?

Of course you do you twat, so make it up to her!'

'I can't it's too late to change the time, the client is a busy guy with plenty of cash and I need the commission on this one. If I don't make the date, I'll lose him to one of the other salesmen, along with the commission and probably my job. I'm not exactly salesman of the month at the moment, and my boss is pressurizing me to "buck up or back out" as he says. Then I'd lose Sarah if I didn't have a job. So I think I'm fucked both ways.'

'Listen Craig' Spike said, 'I'm seeing Kev and Lynn later, I got some of their DVD's and said I would take them back over, so they asked me and Angie to stay and have some supper with them. I'll ask Lynn to ring Sarah and try to help calm her down; they're good mates working together and all, so she'll know what's going on and maybe make the peace for you, eh? Explain things. What do you think?'

'Yeah maybe it's worth a try. Anyway, I got to go and get my shit together ready for this sale, then I can put it right with Sarah tomorrow perhaps.' Craig downed the rest of his beer and walked out the door. 'See ya lads.'

Spike and Danny chatted about Craig for a while, about his moodiness at times and that probably money was the reason behind the couples' problems.

'Right I'm off as well' Spike said, heading for the door. Smiling, he turned 'oh and by the way Danny, your misses prefers dark chocolate before a shag on the bonnet.'

'Fuck off you pervert' Danny replied, hurling the wet dish cloth at him.

Lynn didn't need to call Sarah when Spike and Angie arrived and asked her to, she said they had already been talking at work during their break time and over lunch, so Lynn new all about the problems.

Apparently Craig had been working a lot in the evenings, seeing clients who were out at work all day and could only make late appointments.

She understood that he had to take the arrangements offered; otherwise he wouldn't earn any commission, which was what boosted his income. She was just a bit fed up with their living arrangements mainly, and when she brought it up with Craig, he flew into a rage, they had words, and that was it.

By Thursday evening they had settled their differences, not with chocolates or jewellery, but a kiss and makeup in bed while her parents were out doing the weekly shopping in town. Their lovemaking always seemed better when they were making up after a ruck.

They went to the pub afterwards at about eight thirty, and the others were there when they walked in, so they were greeted with an ear bursting cheer.

Sarah turned a deep shade of scarlet while Craig just smiled and gave them the finger.

Danny gave them drinks on the house, and charged a toast, 'To the happy couple!'

The others joined in, 'The happy couple.'

Later, Dave was stood at the bar with Danny, sharing out the profit from the latest haul of cigarettes, and working out dates for the next lot.

There was a lot of money changing hands, and both of them looked very happy with the arrangements so far.

Dave rejoined the group trying to shove his fat wallet into the pocket of his jeans.

'I'll relieve you of some of that' Karen said, as she pointed at his hip pocket.

'That will pay a couple of our bills out of the way.'

'Yeah ok hun, I was going to hold on to it until we got home. Maybe we can play a little strip poker with it later on eh babe?' He said winking at her.

'Ha . . . a fat chance of that, by the time we get home you'll be too pissed for any kinky sex. You're like a fucking cross channel ferry when you've had a drink . . . roll on and roll off.'

They all laughed.

'If he's the same as Kev' Lynn chirped in, 'he'll fart, try to hold your head under the covers, turn over and two minutes later start snoring for England!'

All the lads cheered.

'Yeah, that's my boy' Said Spike.

The idle banter between the group continued on for a good hour.

'Hey, I just remembered!' said Spike, 'Van Morrison is playing at the Ross-on Wye jazz and folk festival this weekend, we gotta go see him he's great in concert. I think it's about fifteen quid to get in, but I might be able to wangle some free tickets from a mate of mine who does all the stage lighting at the festival . . . are we all up for it then?'

It was a unanimous yes.

'Hey Danny, what about you and Maggie coming along as well? And we can get Billy to pick us up from here with his minibus.'

'I'll check with Maggie, but that sounds great, I know she likes his music, and so do I.'

Danny went off upstairs to see Maggie, and they were both back in the bar a few minutes later.

'Hi guys' Maggie said as she pulled up a chair with the group. 'Danny and I would love to come along with you all, it's about time Danny put his hand in his pocket and took me out for a change, I'll look forward to it, I just love Van The Man Morrison . . . Are you sorting the tickets then Spike?'

'Yeah, no problem, if I can get some free ones we can split the cost of the ones we have to buy, okay?' he said looking around the table. Again everyone was nodding in agreement.

'I'll see Billy Richards and arrange the minibus" said Danny. 'Saturday or Sunday?'

'Let me check with Richie about the freebie tickets first, then I'll let you know tomorrow lunch time okay?' Spike replied.

'Right, that's that then. Now . . . who wants a drink?' asked Danny.

'Are they on the house?' said Kev.

'No, they are on Danny!' said Maggie.

SEVEN.

Sunday 21ˢᵗ June.

Sunday was the day Spike had managed to get the free tickets for, so that evening the group met at the pub and awaited Billy with his fifteen seater mini bus.

He was one minute early when he strolled in and said 'All aboard the skylark,' a phrase he always used which he had picked up from some kiddies TV program.

They all piled into the bus; with four six packs of beer and two litres of wine in screw tops, plus plastic cups for the trip.

An hour later they were inside the arena, having bought five tickets and getting six freebies from Richie. They paid for Billy's ticket because he wouldn't take any petrol money for the trip, but he accepted the free ticket for the show graciously.

Jazz and Folk bands had been playing all day, alternating between the three stages within the arena, and the climax of the day would be Van Morrison on the main centre stage of the arena. He wouldn't be on stage until 10:00 pm, so they had time to move around watching the variety of bands playing. There were souvenir stalls, burger vans and of course a large beer tent at the back of the arena.

They all purchased a black Fedora style hat from a souvenir stall, similar to the one worn by Van Morrison. Everywhere they turned, all that could be seen was a sea of black hatted people, milling around in all directions, all obviously as mad about Van as they were. They watched various performers prior to retiring to the beer tent, and awaiting the main gig.

It was around fifteen minutes before the main event, and people were taking their seats and standing positions ready for the showman to appear. The friends all managed to snatch seats in a six in front five behind formation. That way they could interact together.

The crowd waited in anticipation as the lights dimmed.

Silhouettes of the band members could be seen and it was moments before the great man walked out onto the stage to a huge roar from his fans that were packed in to see him.

The stage lights came up in a myriad of colour, turning it into a glowing furnace. Then the band opened their repertoire with "Brown eyed girl" sending the crowd into a joyous frenzy of singing and dancing in the aisles and sides of the seated areas. Not one person was still, everyone was buzzing.

They continued their set with songs from his greatest hits, songs like "Bright side of the road"; "Gloria"; "Baby please don't go"; "Jackie Wilson said"; "Have I told you lately", and many more.

The show went on into the night. The atmosphere was electric.

He talked to the crowd. He preached to the crowd, and they worshipped him. A religious man dedicated to his beliefs and his music.

A true artiste.

When he asked the crowd to shout out requests, *"She"* was up immediately and calling at him to . . . 'Play Moondance for me.'

He must have heard, because that was his next song.

Yes, Carol was there. The music had awakened her from her subdued state, and Van Morrison was playing her favorite tune, the one she always hummed when she sliced and diced her victims.

The tune was lodged in her head. She was in her element, swaying to and fro to the rhythm of the music.

But still her inner demons were telling her, that more than anything, she needed another victim.

It would have to be soon, very soon.

The pressure in her scull was throbbing, she craved the moment.

Oh Please be soon! Please be very soon!

EIGHT.

'Maggie! Maggie! Can you hear me?'

Danny was shouting above the noise in the arena, to Maggie who had collapsed in the aisle during the performance of "Moondance".

Spike had gone to alert the St Johns Ambulance Brigade, who was quickly on the scene.

They moved her away from the crowd, and across to their treatment tent in the back corner of the arena. Danny and friends followed.

Danny was in the tent with Maggie and the first aiders, the others waited outside.

After being given some quality first aid, she was soon up and about and back to her normal self again.

When she and Danny came out of the tent, she was so embarrassed and couldn't stop apologizing to everyone for spoiling their fun.

They of course told her not to worry. It was very hot in amongst the crowd, and with all the dancing about as well she just got overheated and fainted. No harm done.

The friends all decided to get a drink from the beer tent and stand at the back for the rest of the show, it was a lot cooler there, plus they could pop in and out of the beer tent of course.

Perfect.

After three encores from the band, the fantastic show finished well past midnight.

The crowd moved out from the grounds like a slow flowing river following the contours of a river bank, heading for the vast car park situated at the west end of the park. No fuss, no rush, no fights. That's refreshing.

Once aboard the bus the guys were at first all chatty and excited from the evenings entertainment, but as the homeward trip got underway with Billy's smooth driving, they were all drowsy and nodding off to sleep in no time at all.

Billy was used to this sort of behavior, he didn't mind though. If his passengers were asleep, they wouldn't argue or fight on his bus. Drink can have that effect at any time, even amongst best friends, so sleep was good. He drove them all home safely, humming a tune or two to himself on the way.

NINE.

***

8:00 am. Monday morning 22nd June.

4 weeks since the death of Brian Fielding, the 5th victim, and 49 weeks since the death of Callum Watts, the 1st victim.

In the incident room the new "wall" was taking shape. The time line along the top. A victim photo under the relevant date and time of killing underneath. Below that coloured lines branched out from each of the photos indicating what could be described as a Christmas tree chart of facts. Each team had been adding information to the giant build sheet.

DCI Williams called for the attention of the team.

'Okay guys, I want to run through what we got to date, so if each team talk us through any new info they have and we will take it from there.'

'Barney and Duncan, you can go first.'

Barney stepped up. 'We've been back to employers of each of the "vics", and checked the statements already given. There's nothing different on that score guv. All the victim's guys were fairly decent hard working guys who just enjoyed a night out now and then, sometimes followed with a bit of slap and tickle with a lady of the night.

With one exception. George Pitt—47yrs old. Wife's name is Margaret. He was a factory shift worker on the maintenance section. His workmates all say he would never cheat on his wife, he was very old fashioned and enjoyed a drink with the lads, but when it came to other women it was a definite no no. He is . . . was the only married victim.

The others:-

Callum Watts—33yrs old. Engaged to Jane Woodhouse.

He was a warehouse Fork lift truck driver. Was engaged, but still flirted a lot with girls at work, so his mates were not surprised to hear that he possibly used prostitutes. He had been caught once, luckily it was by a workmate, shagging the secretary at the back of the warehouse in his lunch break.

Michael Grey—42yrs old, single, no evidence of a girlfriend. Was a Supermarket supervisor. He was described as a bit creepy by the women he worked with at the supermarket, and a bit of a computer geek. In fact we have his computer here in the evidence store. The lab boys have found a load of kinky porn sites on it with a lot of "BDSM" jpegs and mpegs in a file. That's "Bondage, Domination and Sado Masochism" photos and film clips for you computer illiterates' said Barney.

'I think we know what it all means' said DS Hayes.

Duncan continued with the report.

'Vince Wallace—40yrs old. Divorced. Driver for the Post Office. Lived on his own in a flat in Cromwell road. Nothing else on him. Again his mates said he liked his free time and just enjoyed life as it came.

Finally, the latest victim . . .

Brian Fielding—37yrs old. Single. No girlfriends. Worked for the local council "Parks & gardens dept". Quiet, good conscientious worker. Very few friends, half a dozen or so, mostly from his local pub "The Howlers Arms". Lived with his sister, brother-in-law and their 2 kids. That's it guv.'

'Okay thanks both . . . just one concern there for me is the fact that George Pitt did not go with other women. Maybe this was just an unlucky one off for him. Let's hold on to that fact for a moment, in fact, Alan . . . let's open a separate list of any strange facts we turn up like this. Put them on that flip chart there will you?' said DCI Williams pointing at a spare one in the corner. 'Right Keith, Sophie what you got?'

'Well guv' Keith started. 'Not a lot to add to the wall as we already know the homes of the "vics". All of which we have gone over with a fine tooth comb.

No differences in the family statements at all.

Margaret Pitt is still very distraught at any idea that her husband would ever go with a prostitute.

Jane Woodhouse has admitted the fact that Callum Watts was probably shagging behind her back.

Michael Grey's brother, Tony, his only relative, knew that Michael was into computers and wasn't surprised that we found the BDSM files on his PC, and that he was having sex with prostitutes.

Vince Wallace's mother didn't believe that her boy would ever associate with the "ladies of the night".

Brian Fielding's sister and brother in law had a good idea that Brian had been with local call girls. He didn't have much else in life.

Sorry guv, but Sophie and I couldn't find anything more than we already have listed.'

'Okay guys, thanks anyway, we just needed to be sure we didn't miss anything.' said the DCI. 'Sharon, Bernie, any luck on your job?'

Sharon began. 'The routines of the victims showed regular patterns of movements. Each had their own little world of fantasy in their spare time.

Again the only odd one out being George Pitt. He was not your regular stop out good time boy. In fact he was the exact opposite. He was not a regular down the local, and generally only went there with the boys if there was something to celebrate . . . say a birthday or something. The night he was killed, he had been for a drink with the lads he worked with to celebrate the birth of a baby girl to one of the electricians on his shift.

George hated being away from his wife for any length of time. They did everything together, holidays with the caravan club up and down the country, green bowling, walking in the Cotswold's and the Forest of Dean was their favorite pastime.

Hobbies and pastimes did not cross over with any of the victims, meaning none played for the same team in anything, say darts or pool for instance. No links there.

On the pub front, they had possibly used the same pub for a drink at some time or other, but there was no positive evidence that showed any two of the victims knowing each other closely. They could have passed in a bar, and that is all. Bernie and I took the photos of all of the victims to each of the locals they used, to see if anyone recognized any of them, nothing doing on that score.

To sum it up, they stuck to their own neighborhood local bars.

That's about it guv, again nothing we didn't already know.'

'Okay, thanks Sharon, Bernie,' said DS Hayes stepping in, 'we'll reallocate new tasks at the end of the reports.'

DCI Williams was stood back looking at "the new wall", he was in deep thought.

'Guv? . . . guv . . . shall we stop for a coffee or do you want to press on?' said the DS.

'What? Oh, yeah umm. Let's take ten, get coffee and keep going.'

While the detectives disappeared to the lads & lassies rooms, then went to fetch coffees from the vending machine, Dicky motioned Alan to come into his office.

He stood at the window with his back to Alan Hayes, who was also a good friend as well as a dedicated colleague; he gazed out to the street below as he talked.

'I don't know where we are going with this Alan' he said. 'The chief is chewing my balls every time I see him. He's demanding a result and we're not anywhere near. We have no witnesses, no murder weapon and no motive. We got fuck all! I'm not saying the guys are not working at it, it's just we don't have a clue.'

My biggest fear is that we won't find anything until this asshole makes a mistake.

That means one thing . . .

It means another corpse, and we can't wait for that. We need some radical thinking to flush this psycho out.'

Alan stood in silence. He had no answer to what the DCI. Was saying. He knew he was right. But he knew the guv'nor needed his support in this crisis.

He spoke up. 'You know everyone in there is loyal to you guv, they look up to you, every last one of them, so you and I are going to lead them on and we are going to crack this case.'

'You're a good friend Al,' said Dicky turning around, 'and a great detective. I wouldn't want anyone else at my side. Thanks for your support mate.'

'Okay then . . . let's get some of that coffee and finish the reports to see where we are then shall we?' said Alan.

TEN.

DS Tim Clark and DC Alan Mclean ran through their report in front of the other detectives who were all looking a bit dejected.

'First off' said Tim 'The scene of crime in each case shows that our attacker appears to hide in wait behind cover of some sort.'

'Can you be more specific Tim?' said Dicky.

'Yes guv, I'll add the info as I go to each "Vic" okay? So, here's the breakdown.' He wrote on the white board next to each victim as he explained.

'Vic 1—Callum Watts. Found in the alleyway off London Road, leading to Christ Church Road. Footprints in the gravel indicate that our attacker was stood behind a wall which would have given adequate cover, at least until the victim was at the point where he was level with the attacker. Also found at the scene and on the victim were synthetic blonde hair strands, probably from a wig worn by the attacker. All valuables and jewellery removed, except for a mobile phone still in his pocket.'

'So our "killer" wears a wig and already has a mobile phone' said Dicky.

'Bear with us guv . . .

Vic 2—George Pitt. Found in the alleyway between Parabola Road and Saint Georges Road. Similar scenario with the position of the attack. The killer had a pillar to step out from as the victim approached. Again synthetic strands of hair found, only this time they were red. All valuables taken. Money and watch. George did not own a mobile phone.'

Al Mclean stepped in to continue with the report—

'Vic 3—Michael Gray. Found just off the main footpath in Sandford Park.

Footprints found at the murder scene, and also behind an adjacent hedgerow where the killer had again apparently laid in wait.'

'So you're saying that we can prove that our killer was hiding from our victims in each case Al?' said Dicky.

'Well I think when you see the entire evidence guv, that it's pretty much consistent for each scene. All valuables taken, with the exception of the mobile phones. This time more blonde strands, forensics say from the same blonde wig as before.'

'Vic 4—Vince Wallace. Found off the Whaddon Road behind the Cheltenham Town Football Club. Another park area. Again the footprints indicate that our killer is in a position off the main footpath where the attack took place, and further prints behind a large bougainvillea bush. All valuables except mobile phone. More strands from the same red wig this time.'

'Vic 5—Brian Fielding. Found . . .'

'Don't tell me' said Dicky, 'In a park, next to a hiding place, no personal effects except a mobile phone . . . and let me guess hair strands from . . . a blonde wig?'

'Dead right guv . . . Pittville Park to be precise, off the main footpath, hedge cover again with more footprints, all valuables gone except mobile phone. Blonde hair strands from the same wig. One other thing guv . . . forensics have estimated from the footprints, that our attacker is approximately 190. lbs and wears size 9 shoes. Also the cuts to each victim indicates our attacker is probably right handed.'

'What's 190. lbs in old money Al?' asked Keith.

'That's about thirteen and a half stone.'

'That's a fucking big lady if you ask me!' said Keith.

Everyone in the room was giving 200% attention; they knew they had some good evidence here.

'Good work guys, we may just have a breakthrough here.' said Dicky.

'Okay, Sgt Hayes and I have been looking at the footage from the funerals and have also come up with nothing. We have found no evidence, of any person, attending more than one of the funerals.

There are no CCTV cameras at any of the crime scenes, but there are nearby cameras within the vicinity to each of the crime sites. So we do need to plough through all of them, and that's going to take time, so I will be asking if we can have some "plods" to do that for us.

So to summarize, Alan can you update our separate chart as we go through this please.' Dicky said to his DS.

'Before we start, I would just like to thank everyone for the extra effort, and hopefully we have something here to give us a small lead in the case . . .

Right, here we go.

Our attacker is:-

- 190. Lbs. or 13½ stone approximately.
- Has size 9 feet.
- Is probably right handed.
- Wears shoulder length Red or Blonde wigs, alternately.
- Takes all the victims' valuables.
- Mobile phones are a no no.?
- Each of the murders, have been committed on either a Thursday or Friday night.
- The kill sites are in no particular pattern around the town, but after the first two murders, it looks like he prefers park area. Probably because it's more open, but has cover areas for him to hide in wait. It gives him the advantage of sighting his prey and also, more escape opportunity should he be cornered.'

'You said *he* guv?' said Sgt Hayes.
'What was that?'
'You said *he*.'

'Well, I'm willing to bet a pound to a pinch of shit, that our killer is a man!' Said Dicky. 'Size nines and one hundred and ninety pounds! Like Keith said earlier, that's a big woman! So . . . any takers?

Well I think referring to our serial killer as a he isn't wrong, but we still need to keep an open mind.'

Everyone in the room was nodding in agreement with his deductions.

It did seem pretty obvious, although there was no substantial proof as yet, so yes they would have to keep an open mind.

'So . . . here's what we're going to do next' said Dicky.

ELEVEN.

The evening of Thursday 25th June.

Its 7:00 pm. Craig and Dave are having a drink with Danny in "The Empty Jug" bar, chatting about their day. At around seven fifteen, Spike joined them, he immediately got them laughing with a joke or two.

'Hey, did you hear the one about Paddy jumping off a cliff with a chicken under each arm? he told his wife he was taking up "Hen Glidin" . . .

His mate Mickey, jumped out of an aeroplane with a parrot and a shotgun . . . he was trying out "Parrot shoot jumpin".'

The guys were laughing as Maggie appeared from behind the curtain to the back room, she had overheard the jokes.

'Which kiddies magazine did you get those jokes from "The Beano"?' she said with a grin.

'No, I think it was "Take a break" magazine actually. So . . . what's happening then?' said Spike.

'Not much' said Craig, 'I'm off to check out another rich client shortly, could be another good payday as long as I can get the sale!'

'Well I have an appointment as well later,' said Dave rubbing his soft unworkman-like hands together, looking at Danny and giving him the wink.

'So what time do you expect to be back here then Dave?' asked Danny.

'Not sure mate, I might leave it until tomorrow night to save me rushing back, you know!'

They were of course talking about the illegal tobacco that Dave had coming over from France this evening. Dave would always collect outside of the depot in case of prying eyes. It was a risky thing he and Danny had going, and the rewards were rich pickings, but they would be up shit creek without a paddle if they got caught.

'Where's your meeting then Craig?' Spike suddenly asked.

'What?' Said Craig, who was away with the fairies, and looked spooked by the question.

'The m-e-e-t-i-n-g, you know, tonight?'

'Oh . . . yeah, you mean the appointment with the client?'

'Duh . . . yeah!' said Spike mockingly.

'It's . . . umm over in . . . Worcester, yeah Worcester.'

'Well you don't sound too sure!' said Dave.

'Yep I'm sure' said Craig appearing to wake up from his trance. Glancing at his watch he said 'In fact I better make a move, don't want to be late do I?'

With that he downed what was left in his glass, and walked out without another word.

'What's up with him then?' Said Kev who was just coming in, sidestepping out of the way of Craig, who was on his way out through the door like a man on a mission.

'Dunno!' said Danny 'Seems in a funny mood tonight, maybe he and Sarah are at loggerheads again—what're you having Kev?'

'Oh thanks mate, I'll just have an orange juice' said Kev.

'Hey . . . this ain't a free fucking bar you know!' Danny chirped.

'Yeah I know Dan . . . Give us a bag of roasted nuts as well will ya? Any of you guys want another drink?' He said to Dave and Spike.

'I'll have a half' Said Spike.

'No thanks Kev' said Dave 'I've got to get going as well in a minute.—So what's with the OJ, on the wagon are we?'

'I've got a grading at the "dojo" tonight, some of my students are ready to move up a belt so I can't stay long, and it's not very good smelling of beer, sitting alongside other judges who are teetotal!'

'Christ it's going to be like a morgue in here shortly, all you lot pissing off elsewhere! You're staying aren't you Spike?'

'Nuh, sorry Dan I've a job on tonight before I have another drink.'

Within minutes the three buddies had drank up and were gone. Danny and Maggie were alone behind the bar. There was only "old Bertie", who sat in his usual corner sipping his stout and reading the evening edition of "The Cheltenham Echo", and the young couple who had been sitting quietly at the end of the bar for the last hour or so.

The couple had just finished their drinks and were also about to leave.

Outside as they walked away from the pub towards where they had parked their car, DC Sharon Simmons and DC Bernie Webb were discussing the conversations that they had just overheard in "The Empty Jug".

Sharon had discreetly taken photos of each person in the bar, with the use of her mobile phone camera, whilst pretending to text someone.

The other detectives were also paired up to do the same in other selected pubs around the city, and back at the incident room they would download the photos to a computer. The photos would be printed off and put up for show on a board with their names alongside, any known villains or persons with a police record who were identified, would immediately be pulled in for questioning. Also any other links to the victims would be entered on the information board. Some details of the conversations were also included on the board to help place the individuals for that evening. As yet these characters had committed no known crimes.

This was only the first phase of the evening's operation, as set up by DCI Williams, he had a gut instinct that the killer was going to strike again soon because of the decreasing time between the attacks. So he was trying to cover all bases by patrolling for the next two nights, in case the killer struck again.

Phase two was to commence this same evening at 9:00 pm.

TWELVE.

9:30 pm in Carol's flat above the launderette.

She was putting on make-up and getting ready for the kill.

She knew it had only been about 4 or 5 weeks since the last night out, but the adrenaline was pumping and she needed to get it out of her system tonight. A couple more shots of vodka would help while she completed her make up.

By ten thirty she was driving her car to the selected spot for tonight's entertainment, and twenty minutes later she was parked in a quiet dark side road, only a five minute walk to her destination.

She sat in the car; one last check in the rearview mirror to make sure the red wig was secured properly. Then she turned off the interior light, and waited for her eyes and senses to adjust to the night. She removed the scalpel from her shoulder bag, which was on the passenger seat next to her, and held it up in front of her, then she pulled off the protective sheath and sat twisting it in her hand, mesmerized by the glinting surgical steel.

After replacing the sheath, and putting the knife back in her bag, she then removed a new pair of surgical gloves and put them on. She took out her mobile phone and turned it off, then put it in the glove-box of the car. She didn't want any distractions.

It was 10:55 pm., and she was ready.

She got out of the car, locked it then started walking, the blood was surging through her veins and pumping that adrenaline around.

The voice in her head was saying—'not long now.' Her mind was set, relief would come soon!

Windyridge green was situated at the end of Windyridge Road, a small play park and gardens, with a cricket pitch in the middle, and a football pitch at one end.

It had six or so entrances and exits. A perfect shortcut home for the late night drinkers on the estate.

She entered the park and scanned the area for the perfect location. Yes, up ahead to the right about 50 meters, the path turned slightly and had good cover to the side in the form of a hedgerow running parallel to the pathway, and separating off a piece of garden from the path. She could wait at the end of the hedge for an unsuspecting victim.

She moved into position, trying to compose herself.

Time passed slowly, drinking her energy. Her mouth was dry, and a shot of vodka would help.

'No . . . overcome the negative thoughts, stay focused' she told herself. She was becoming frantic with the thought of not claiming a victim tonight, so she began to hum her song, "Moondance" from the Van Morrison album.

It had a calming effect.

There was only a half moon in the sky tonight, and it was hiding behind heavy cloud cover, there was also a smell of rain in the air.

11:50 pm. *'He will come! He will come!'* She kept telling herself.

More humming . . .

11:55 pm. her prayers were answered.

The anxiety lifted and she was calmed by the approach of her prey.

Just as the rain started, Peter Sherman entered through the same gateway that Carol had some 50 minutes or so earlier. He wobbled as he walked, the seven or so pints that he had drunk that evening at the "Moonraker", his local pub, had given him the desired effect.

He neither desired a woman at this moment, nor was he in a fit state to shag anything anyway, he wanted to get home to bed. Sleep was what he desired, nothing else.

He was now only twenty metres away.

Carol took out the scalpel, and carefully removed and dropped the sheath back in her shoulder bag. The knife in her hand ready. She was sizing up the target ready for the strike.

He was about five feet eight and medium build, slight beer belly. Not a problem, she would slice through him like a hot knife through butter. She would have to step across him, because he was coming from her left side, and being right handed she always cut from her right to left. Again no problem, she would merely step out in front of him, then an extra step to her right would suffice for her to perform the perfect cut. He was wearing a thin jacket which would not make any difference.

Ten metres now and he suddenly stopped, he was fumbling in his jacket pocket for a packet of cigarettes, and then, finally managing to get one out he attempted to light it.

After being successful on the third attempt, he then accidentally dropped the packet on the floor and cussed out loud.

'Fuck it!'

He almost fell forward onto his head as he bent forward to pick it up, then he stood there savoring the first draw on the cancer stick, making the end glow brilliant orange. He pulled up the collar on his windbreaker jacket against the cold rain, which was now coming down quite heavy.

Five metres away now.

Carol stepped out from behind the hedge nearly scaring the bloke to death. He stopped mid track. She took the extra step to her right, ready, scalpel held down by her side. She was in position.

The rain had flattened her wig to her head, her mascara and other face make-up was beginning to run down her face in coloured rivulets, she had mud all over her shoes and looked like she had been dragged through a hedge backwards. She looked more like a clown who had just had a bucket of water thrown over its head.

'What the fuck!!!' The man said, eyes wide with shock, 'Stupid bitch, you frightened the shit outta me, what the fuck do you want, fuck off home!'

He just stood there, waiting for her to move out of his way, but she was just staring at him, humming some goddamn tune that he thought he knew.

She knew this was going to be different, because this man was not going to do as she expected.

Things were not going to plan. She would have to improvise.

'Don't you want me?' she said provocatively.

'Do I fuck!' The man slurred, 'I just want to get home to bed.'

He took another deep draw on his cigarette and blew the smoke out through his nostrils.

He saw her face suddenly change, contorting at his abusive reply. Her make-up was changing into colours of the rainbow and running down her face, it made her look like something inhuman.

She started forward towards him, and he saw a glint of something in her hand so he stepped back out of fear.

The cigarette dropped from his fingers to the floor, and his jaw dropped as he suddenly realized something.

He had flashing memories of the report in the papers about a psycho killer on the loose.

This couldn't be her surely? Could it?

His legs went to jelly as she continued toward him. She had to strike now because he had seen the knife.

This could be messy!

'Whoa . . . wait a minute!' he pleaded.

THIRTEEN.

He was backing away now, his legs still making it hard for him to move, it was hard enough walking forward half pissed, let alone backwards!

He finally stumbled, falling backwards onto his rear end and then he was trying to do the crab walk backwards on the pathway, even more difficult than walking backwards!!!

'Why me?????' He shouted.

'Because I want you!' she said, showing him the blade and smiling with a smudged lipstick mouth, making her look like some weird obsessed freak.

He was becoming more sober by the second. What do I do? He was thinking.

Panic rose in his throat **'HELP ME!!!!'** He screamed. **'HELP ME!!!'**

The fear factor was activating his self preservation instincts.

She was laughing hysterically now, looking down as she stood astride him.

Then, her face suddenly took on a menacing look, and he knew she was about to strike.

Pete was now as sober as he could ever be, he knew he only had one chance and that was going to be a slim one.

Before she could get low enough to cut him, he drove his right foot upwards as hard as he could and toe punted her dead centre of her crutch. Bull's-eye!

A loud guttural sound exploded from her angry mouth as his size ten "Timberland boot" struck home. She dropped the knife and clutched both hands to her crutch, and at the same time as she started to drop to her knees, he made a grab for her hair so that he could drag her to the side of him and escape. But the wig came off in his hand and she landed on top of him.

Her voice had changed to that of a wounded animal, and Pete realized that his actions had only made the situation worse.

They were now face to face, and Pete could see into the crazed eyes of his attacker who was now only inches from his own face. The spoilt make-up was running down her face, along with the tears of pain caused by the boot in the groin, and then a long stream of expletives flowed from her distorted mouth . . .

'You fuckpig! you bastard!, you cunt!, you won't get away. You're destined to die tonight. You have to die tonight!'

The kick to the groin must have been excruciatingly painful, but the attacker who had come down on top of him, was now rolling off him and clawing towards the knife.

Pete quickly rolled the other way and was just about on his feet, when he felt the burning slice of the blade across the back of his thigh.

He dropped to one knee as though someone had chopped his leg off. The pain was indescribable; it was nothing he had ever felt before. He too cried out loud in pain and shouted abuse at his attacker. But he knew he could not give up trying to escape now, because he would surely die.

'HELP ME! . . . HELP ME!' he screamed out again.

Gripping the back of his thigh with one hand, he somehow managed to crawl several metres away from the crazy knife wielding maniac, but knew he would not get very far. The madwoman was recovering quickly from the kick, and would have no trouble catching a one legged man. She was in fact already on her feet, and seemed to be gathering her things and looking at the ground around for something, but appeared to give up on what she had dropped and was now refitting and straightening the red wig, staring at Pete with wild eyes.

Pete was now dragging his blood soaked leg behind him. With his hands on the ground, he was doing a forward three legged crab race against the clock, and along the wet path. He knew his time was nearly up. The killer had composed herself again, and although the pain in her groin was still causing her to feel nauseas, her task was not yet complete. She would overcome the pain and move on towards the wounded victim so that she could finish the kill.

Pete was now getting weaker, he had lost a lot of blood and was beginning to feel dizzy, he could just lie down and go to sleep.

The attacker was coming at him now, but he had no fight left in him.

He was going to die!

He lay down on his back, feeling the cold rain popping on his face. The crazy person with the glinting knife in hand, was once again standing over him, this time guarding against another kick, no more mistakes!

No more kicks to the groin!

The last thing Pete heard before passing out, was this crazy woman humming that tune, "Moondance", yes that was the tune! Then he thought he heard other voices in the distance, but he couldn't be sure, he just needed to close his eyes.

The voices Peter had heard were the shouts from DC Sharon Simmons, and DC Bernie Webb, as they were running hard towards what appeared to be an attacker and someone lying on the ground.

The rain was coming down heavy now and obscured their vision. 'Hey you, stop right there!' they shouted as they ran from the opposite side of the park, attempting to cut across the cricket pitch, but the grass was very slippery and they had a hard time keeping a foothold.

The killer saw them coming, and knew she could outrun them by taking the pathway back the way she came in, but before she set off, she looked down at her victim, thinking should she cut the carotid artery to confirm her MO.

She decided quickly, that the man on the ground may be faking, and could grab and hold her until these interfering bastards arrived, so she quickly plunged the knife into the man's abdomen, then she ran off into the night, making her escape.

Sharon and Bernie split up, Sharon ran towards the victim, shouting into her radio as she struggled to keep her footing, while Bernie set off on a tangent after the attacker.

Bernie was slipping and sliding on the grass, and he fell onto his knees more than once and knew he was not going to catch the attacker, who had already reached the exit gate and was off into the darkness.

When he finally got to the gate, there was no sign of anyone up or down the street, it was pointless running either way, as he had no idea which direction the attacker had gone. He decided it was safer not to, in case the attacker was waiting for him in an alley, so he turned back towards where Sharon was attending to the victim on the ground.

He could see her frantic movements over him as he ran back to where she was trying desperately to stop him bleeding. She had found the knife wound to the gut, and was applying pressure to that, but blood was still pouring onto the rain soaked pathway from another wound. The rain water mixing with the blood, had turned the ground red and into what looked like a scene from a massacre.

'Just keep the pressure on that wound Sharon, he must have another wound somewhere else, I'll try to find it' said Bernie.

A minute passed before he located the slash to the thigh muscle. He quickly removed the belt from his own trousers and strapped it as tight as he could around the mans leg above the wound. The blood letting appeared to be stemmed, for now at least.

Sharon had managed to radio the back up team as she approached the person on the ground, so they should be only minutes away now.

Bernie got back on the radio, emphasizing the emergency call for an ambulance to attend urgently.

The man on the ground was barely alive; he had lost a lot of blood and was in and out of conciousness. He was not responding to Sharon and Bernie as they attempted to try and keep him conscious.

'Shit!' said Sharon, 'a minute earlier and we would have had the bastard!'

'Dicky is going to go ape shit' said Bernie.

'Yeah—well lets hope this poor sod survives, then maybe we will have some info to work with, otherwise that'll be another score to the slasher.'

Moments later flashing lights lit up the park like a funfair, and noisy sirens echoed around the ground transforming the quiet area into a party for voyeurs.

People were coming out of the woodwork to see what all the commotion was about. At the scene within five minutes, there were police, paramedics, photographers, and ambulance chasers, those who follow to get a story from someone else's misfortune.

Local people were being held back from the crime scene by uniformed officers. The place was manic. Within half an hour the whole team were there and had split up to search the neighborhood for any signs of the attacker, but they knew it was pointless, she would be long gone by now, but DCI Williams was in no mood to take no for an answer.

Sharon and Bernie had given a brief account to DCI Williams of what had happened earlier, he was not impressed.

He wanted a full account of movements from 21:00 hrs to the current moment, in writing on his desk by 09:00hrs Friday morning.

SOCO (scenes of crime officers), were now on the scene and taping off the area where the attack had taken place. All they could hope for was that the crime scene had not been compromised by the amount of people milling around, as well as the rain.

Two uniform officers were assigned to go with the victim, their instructions was not to allow anyone near him other than medical staff at the hospital. He was still alive but in a critical condition.

It was going to be another long night!

FOURTEEN.

Carol was back in her flat above the launderette, she was seething with anger. She tore off her clothes and threw them across the room, poured herself a large vodka and slugged it down in one.

She poured another and sat down on her chair to gather her thoughts. '**Fuck it!**' she shouted aloud.

'Those bastards ruined it,' she said to herself, *'why couldn't they mind their own business and I could have been satisfied, but no, someone always has to spoil it by sticking their nose into things that don't concern them . . . Fuckpigs! That's what they are . . . Fuckpigs! I'll just have to show them nosey bastards who they're messing with.'*

She showered and dressed, then after putting all the wet clothes in a bin bag, she tied them up and put the bag in the corner. She put the cheap necklace and one earring on the top of the chest of drawers. She had been careless enough to lose one of the clip on earrings during the struggle; no matter, it was only untraceable junk that could be bought at any open market stall or car boot sale for pennies.

She sat back down on the chair, elbows on knees holding the vodka glass in one hand and the bottle in the other. Taking sips from the half full glass, her thoughts replayed step by step the events of the evening, trying to establish what went wrong.

'Maybe I stepped out in front of the man too soon which made the attack that much more difficult? Maybe it was the wrong location' the guy was the wrong type he wasn't interested in prostitutes so that had a big influence on the events that followed. If the interfering couple hadn't turned up I could have finished him properly, and would have been satisfied. What was the couple doing there anyway? Were they having kinky sex in the park or just passing through? No matter, they wouldn't be able to recognize me.'

She suddenly sat upright. *'What if the guy didn't die after I left him? he saw my face and would definitely be able to give a description . . .* 'no way,' she said aloud, convincing herself that he was almost dead when she plunged the knife into his gut, he would have bled out in no time at all.

'*No, he's dead alright, only not the way he was supposed to die. It didn't satisfy me, **and I need to be satisfied** . . . Carol needs to be satisfied, it's my duty.'*

Downing the slug of vodka she said out loud to herself, 'Tomorrow . . . tomorrow I will fulfill my promise!'

She put the bottle on the chest of drawers and the glass in the sink.

After a quick shower and a change of clothes she checked the back door was locked securely, picked up her keys from the little table and turned out the lights. She left through the front door, closing it until she heard the clunk of the latch, then she calmly walked back to where she had parked the car.

She checked her mobile phone and saw that she had 2 missed calls.

'Shit that may take some explaining'; nevertheless she drove home thinking about tomorrow.

FIFTEEN.

Friday 26th June.

9:00 am.,

Bernie and Sharon handed over their report to DCI Williams. He put it down on the top of other reports on his overflowing desk. He was a little more controlled now after a few hours sleep, more sleep than Sharon and Bernie had managed after staying up most of the night, trying to get the facts together about their stakeout mishap typed up into a report.

What they hadn't been totally truthful about, was that when the rain started they took cover under the cricket pavilion roof which overhung on the far side, where they would not have had a view across the park.

'I hope for your sakes that fella pulls through, or we are all gonna get stuffed by the chief this time!' He said, looking up from a report he was writing.

Sharon started to explain . . . 'Guv we were . . .'

'Not now!—We'll go over it in the incident room. We need to detail all the facts in sequence and I want everyone to hear, so save your story for the meeting at nine thirty. Now go and get some coffee and be ready to answer any questions from the team.'

He dismissed them with the wave of his hand and continued writing his press release. They both got coffee and walked into the chit chat in the incident room. The rest of the team was there, drinking their coffee and awaiting the wrath of Dicky. But the chit chat mood was clearly upset by the presence of Sharon and Bernie, as if it was their fault for everything.

The room fell silent.

Looking around the faces in the room Bernie spoke out.

'What's this? Are Sharon and I accused of the murder of five and the attempted murder of one? Come on guys, we did our best out there last night! Any one of you could have been in our position and could have done no more than we did. So cut this blame shit and give us the support a team should—We would for anyone of you!'

A few faces changed to that of agreement, a few didn't. They would have to prove to their colleagues that they did everything that they possibly could have done under the circumstances.

DCI Williams and DS Hayes entered at 9:28 am.

Dicky calmly began the debrief.

'Well, quite a night we had eh? I've received all your reports from the blanket stakeouts we operated last night, thank you all for that. Obviously the only one that means anything will be Bernie and Sharon's, as they were on the scene of the latest attack . . .

Now, I have just read their full report and, I want to thank them both for doing exceptionally well under the difficult circumstances that they had to deal with last night.'

Sharon and Bernie were both surprised at the positive comments from the guv'nor, but there was a loud groan of disagreement in the room from some of the detectives.

'Hold on, hold on!' Said Dicky. 'I want you to hear them out for yourselves. I wouldn't normally make them do this, but I think you'll appreciate the difficult stakeout they had if you hear it from them.

Are you okay with doing it this way Bernie? Sharon?' He looked at them both as he asked.

They both nodded in agreement. 'Sure guv' . . . 'Yes guv.'

Bernie stepped out to the front of the detectives. Sharon perched herself on the edge of a desk close by, ready to back up her partner with his report to the team.

He started.

'At approximately nine pm, Sharon and I entered "Windyridge Green" park and due to our unfamiliarity of the park, we decided to stroll around the perimeter to study the layout and best possible option for cover should our man chose this location.

On doing so we realized how vast the area of cover was. Although classed as a small park compared to say "Pittville", it is still a reasonable size area. It has a football pitch, a cricket pitch and pavilion, a small car park area, and a small children's play park, swings and things. Then there are sections of border gardens with bushes dotted around the perimeter pathway.

The park also has six entrances/exits, some have swing gates others don't. The larger gate to the car park area was locked with a chain and padlock.

To enable us to choose the best viewing cover in the park we walked around the perimeter path three times. We decided the pavilion would give us best cover but obscured our view in the one direction, so we would have to move position every so often to check the other view across the park.'

'Tell us about the people you saw while you were there Bernie' said Dicky.

'May I?' said Sharon stepping up.

'Sure' said Dicky. 'Please continue.'

'We entered the park from the opposite end to the cricket pavilion when we arrived. Then, as we were walking towards it, we heard a commotion in the shadows, and we could hear voices. We both approached with care in case it was our attacker, only to find a young couple going at it against the pavilion doors!'

A few of the detectives sniggered at the thought of it.

'Okay okay' said Dicky. 'Go on Sharon?'

'Well, Bernie and I quickly pulled out our badges and moved them on. The young stud was pretty pissed off at us interrupting his, what shall I say? Enjoyment, and gave us a bit of verbal before they moved off. That was shortly after arriving, so say nine ten pm.

As Bernie said, we did three laps of the park and decided the pavilion was our best viewpoint option.'

'Tell us about the other people you saw' said Dicky.

'On the second lap we passed another young couple out for a stroll. When they passed us, we stopped near a bush a bit further on and pretended to have a kiss and cuddle so that Bernie could watch their movements. They just went out of the next exit they came to. The time would now have been about nine forty five.

We carried on strolling at a slow pace. It was taking us about twenty minutes per lap, because we didn't want to draw attention to ourselves by racing around. We wanted to look like an average couple out for an evening chat and a walk.

Finally after circulating back to the pavilion, we settled at what we called position 1 of the 2 needed to view the whole park area.

At precisely ten thirty five, we were passed at the pavilion by a jogger in full track suit, it could have been blue or black with a white stripe down each of the sleeves and leggings. He was wearing a pair of Nike trainers, a blue or black Nike bobble hat, without the bobble. I think they call them "beanie hats". He also had earphones on, so probably an iPod or something like that. He was clean shaven, and we could just make out dark collar length hair below his hat. We spotted him approaching and pretended to be otherwise engaged as he passed. He did have a quick look back as he rounded the top of the field about thirty metres from us.

We didn't see which gate he came in, but we watched him leave by the same exit as our attacker did later that evening. He may have entered by that gate and did a full circuit of the park; he looked like someone who was in serious training, especially being out running at that time of night.

He was about the same height and weight that our forensic guys estimated from the previous crime scenes.'

'So are you suggesting that this jogger could be our man doing a recce of the park before he returns for the kill?' asked DS Hayes.

'Always a possibility' said Bernie.

'I agree' said Dicky, 'it's a perfect way of checking the area, and to pick a spot where to lay in wait. Okay, those were the only people you saw before the actual attack on this guy correct?'

'That's right' said Sharon.

'So you're saying that you didn't see the attacker enter the park?'

'No guv' . . . 'as we said, our lookout point did have a blind spot, so she must have entered when we were facing away from her position.'

'But even when you were facing that way, you still couldn't see anyone lurking? In particular the attacker?'

'No guv.'

'So she was obviously fairly well concealed?'

'I guess so guv.'

'Okay, let's go over what happened next then.'

Bernie continued.

'The time was around midnight when we thought we could hear what sounded like shouts for help coming from the far side of the park. The rain was coming down hard and we had our hoods up, so the sounds were muffled.

As we moved around the pavilion to our 2nd preferred position, we could see two people, one was laid out on the pathway, and the other was standing alongside.'

'So what you're saying' said the DCI, 'is that you also missed the victim entering the park?'

'Yes guv.'

'Okay, continue.'

'We started running towards them and were shouting at the person standing over the other to stop where he was. The next thing that happened was that we saw the attacker strike quickly downwards at the guy on the floor, and as we found out later that the person standing had stabbed the other in his gut.

He then ran off towards the exit that our jogger had used earlier. I've been saying he, but as we got closer to the scene where the attacker was running from, it became clear that it was a woman running away.

We split up, and Sharon ran towards the guy that was down and I chased after the attacker. I lost my footing a couple of times due to the wet grass and by the time I reached the pathway, she was gone out of sight. I decided not to go any further, I had no idea of her direction of escape, so I headed back to Sharon and helped her to stem the blood loss from the victims' injuries.

By this time he was lying in a bloody pool and I called again for the ambulance and so on . . . then you guys were on the scene.'

'Okay, thanks Bernie . . . Sharon. So lets pick the bones out of that while we wait for SOCO`s report, it should be in shortly' said Dicky, 'I asked them to move quickly while the trail is hot.'

Just then the door opened and a uniformed officer walked in and handed a note to DCI. Williams.

'It's news from the hospital sir.' he said, and walked back out of the room.

SIXTEEN.

The headlines of "The Cheltenham Echo" Friday 26ᵗʰ June late evening edition read . . .

"Another knife attack Death" . . . A police spokesman said, 'that a man was viciously attacked and fatally wounded in Windyridge Park last night as he walked home from a public house at around midnight. The victim had spent the evening drinking with friends after finishing a late shift at his workplace. It appears that on leaving the public house, he was walking his usual route home through the park when he was attacked. He was single and lived alone in Council accommodation.' The mans identity has been withheld temporarily at the request of his family, who were in shock and not available for comment.

The police spokesman also said, 'A young couple had tried to help the man who was attacked, administering resuscitation until the ambulance they had called arrived. Unfortunately he never regained conciousness and it was reported that he died on the way to hospital.'

The attacker, a young woman, was seen running away from the scene by the couple.

The Police say that it is possible that she may be a local girl, but do not know of any reason behind the attack. The couple who assisted the victim, said that they had been out for a walk in the park, and when they heard shouts for help saw a woman running away from where the man was badly injured on the ground. They called for an ambulance and tried to give first aid to the man.

Police are not treating this attack in connection to the serial killer currently terrorizing Cheltenham.

Meanwhile Investigations are continuing.

Anyone who may have information about this crime please contact CID at the Gloucestershire Police HQ.

'Stupid fuckers couldn't even get the description right!' Thought Carol, as she sat in her car reading the headlines of the newspaper. *'Twats! Next time I will make sure they know who they are dealing with. Tonight I will show them, they won't be expecting it so soon. I will really give them something to think about!'*

SEVENTEEN.

Earlier that afternoon around five thirty at Cheltenham General Hospital, DCI Williams and DS Hayes were sitting at the bedside of the latest victim.

His name was Peter Sherman.

He had spent many hours in surgery, and due to the skills of the surgeons, had pulled through despite a major blood loss, extensive damage to his bowel, spleen, and the severed muscle, nerves and arteries in his thigh.

He had survived and would be a key witness, but at the moment he was still in a critical condition, passing in and out of conciousness, so they were unable to get a statement from him yet.

DCI Williams had given the press a false report earlier that day, with the permission of Peter Sherman's family, his father and sister. He fabricated a story that the stabbing had been fatal.

He believed the attack had been that of the serial killer, even though the M.O. was slightly different, but he had put that down to her being disturbed in the act by his officers.

Dicky knew he would probably face some sort of disciplinary action when the chief got wind of his fake statement to the press, but he wanted the killer to believe that she had succeeded, and believe that her identity was reasonably intact, hence the lack of detail. Luckily, Dicky knew that the chief was away until Wednesday, he was on a seminar somewhere in the Cotswold's, so it gave him and his team a few days to get ahead on the case.

By pretending that Peter was dead, he thought it might pacify the killer, making her think she had succeeded in her killing spree, even though the witnesses description were vague, she might come round to thinking that she had fooled the police again.

If the killer knew that her last victim was still alive, she may be tempted to strike again immediately or attempt to finish him off at the hospital.

Dicky wanted his witness safe, and this would give the squad a bit of breathing time.

Peter Sherman's father and sister live two doors away from him in the same council block of flats. The mother had died a year ago, and it was shortly after that when Peter moved into his own flat. The family were more than happy to cooperate with DCI Williams and his false story to the newspapers, and would remain unavailable for comment until the detective had sufficient detail to work with.

Back at the incident room, the detectives were going through the events, and working over the current information still piecing it together. They were particularly interested in the movements of a few people from whose conversations had been overheard in the pubs. It may add up to nothing, but they knew they had to follow up on any lead they could find. It was another long shot, but the general feeling of the team was that this person had to be a local, so there was a good chance that he or she would be a drinker in a local pub at some time or other.

Maybe just one of the conversations overheard by the detectives would come up trumps. They would certainly find out soon. The pairs were going to visit the same public houses as before, only this time not undercover, they were going in to question the locals, and follow up on where people were.

DC Barney Miller and DC Duncan Montgomery headed out for the "Moonraker", Peter Sherman's local.

As they walked into the bar, they sensed the menacing mood of the twelve or so people, mainly men, who were there drinking and talking about the headlines in the newspaper. There were a few people who were angry about their friends' death, even though it was still not confirmed to them that it was Peter Sherman, some of the locals had already tried to contact Peter and had worked it out.

The police asking questions about him more or less confirmed it to them. It was difficult asking questions about a man who was supposed to be dead when all along he was recovering, so they had to be very precise in their technique, giving away as little as possible about the circumstances. They needed to quickly confirm the drinkers' alibis. The landlord was a genuine publican who didn't want trouble at his door, so he was eager to confirm that the guys who were drinking there that night, were all there until well after Peter left. There were no single women in on the night either.

Barney and Monty were quite sure the killer did not reside in this pub.

DC Keith Butler and DC Sophie Smith were checking out "The Landsman Inn", from the names of punters who were drinking that night, they had one follow up to do, two others had checked out ok. Again no single women in that night.

They had an address of the man in question and were soon on the way to pay him a visit.

A middle aged unkempt woman, with a cigarette hanging from her mouth answered the door, and welcomed them with 'Ha . . . the police I take it? What the fuck do you want? My old man ain't here if that's who you're after!'

'May we come in, we do have a few questions that you may be able to answer about your husband' said Sophie showing her I.D. badge.

'If you must!' she said, leading them into the kitchen. 'I suppose you want a cupper tea then?'

Looking around the grubby kitchen, the sink full of yesterday's dirty pots and pans, and not a clean space anywhere, they both answered in unison 'No thanks.'

'Can you tell us where your husband was last night Mrs Hardy?'

'How do you know my name?' she snapped.

'Your husbands name is Tom Hardy correct? . . . So?'

'Well, yeah okay . . . he went up the pub.'

'What time did he go out?'

'Go out! . . . he didn't come home from work, he went straight to the pub as usual, got in about eleven thirty, pissed as a fart, fell on the sofa and slept there till he went to work at eight this morning.'

'Is this his regular pattern then?' Asked Sophie as she jotted notes on her pad.

'Yep, same old.'

'What about tonight then? Down the pub again is he?' Asked Keith knowing full well that he wasn't there earlier.

'No, he went on his weekend long haul this morning, I won't see him now until Sunday night when he gets back from France . . . he's a lorry driver you know, local during the week and a long haul at weekends, he gets more money for that you see.'

'Sounds like you don't spend a lot of time together Mrs. Hardy?' Said Sophie.

'No, thank fuck, he's outta my hair most of the time, a pain in the arse is what he is!'

'Well thank you Mrs. Hardy, that's all for now, we'll be on our way then.' Said Keith.

'Sure you won't stay for a cuppa? I was beginning to enjoy our little chat, I don't get to see many people around here ya know!'

'Maybe another time.' Said Sophie as she followed Keith quickly down the path.

Another dead end.

EIGHTEEN.

DS Tim Clark and DC Alan Mclean were sitting in the "Westchester Arms" drinking coke. The place was empty except for an old couple in the corner sipping halves of lager and eating cheese toasties.

They had already spoken to the landlord, who said that there had been a few single women in that night, but they had left with a gang of blokes who were going to a nightclub.

Tim and Mac were waiting for four other lads to come in. The landlord said they always came in around seven and had a few drinks together on a Friday.

It was ten past seven before the first one showed up. Tim and Mac called him over to their table and checked his comings and goings the night before. They told him that they were making enquiries into a theft.

He said that the four of them had gone from the "Westchester" straight to a night club called "Cleo's" on "The Promenade".

He said they were regulars, and that the bouncer on the door would confirm that they were there till two am.

'And his name would be?' Said Mac.

'Stu . . . Stuart Wiggins, a big black fella.'

Minutes later, two more of the group came in together, and from the bar they looked across to where Tim and Mac were talking to their mate.

'Hey, what's up Steve?' said the one called Mike.

'These fella's are cops, want to know where we were last night.'

'And why's that then?' said Mike.

'We're investigating a theft in this area last night . . . where's your other friend?' said Mac.

'Who Jeff, he's got a ceiling to plaster, said he'd be in later about eight.'

'So you were all in "Cleo's Club" till what time?' said Tim looking towards Ashley, the other guy at the bar.

'Bout two am' said Ashley with attitude. 'Problem?'

'No, that's fine!' said Mac 'We'll want to talk to . . . who was it? Jeff? Later.'

'Yeah, Jeff Markham' said Steve.

'Here' said Mac, handing Steve a note pad, 'Can you write down his address on there for us? . . . cheers!'

Tim and Mac finished their cokes and headed for the door. Tim said 'Thanks guys, maybe see you later!'

He heard Ashley say 'Not if we see you fuckin pigs first!'

Tim stopped to turn back towards the lads, but Mac caught his arm . . . 'leave it mate, we'll sort it later.'

Meanwhile, Bernie and Sharon were talking to Danny and Maggie Lewis at "The Empty Jug" when Spike and Dave walked in.

'Hey Dave, I didn't know that Dan and Mags were turning this into a "Swingers bar" did you?' They both saw the funny side until Danny said.

'This is detectives Simmons and Webb, they're investigating a theft in the area.'

Spike and Dave both turned a shade of scarlet. 'Shit . . . sorry guys, no offence' said Spike.

'Oh, don't mind Spike' Maggie directed at Sharon, 'He's always taking the piss.'

'No problem' said Sharon, looking towards Spike puckering her lips and giving a wink, 'I can give as good as I take . . . Spikey.'

Spike turned a deeper shade of scarlet.

'Just a few questions please' said Bernie. 'Where were you last night around midnight?'

'Shaggi . . . uh, in bed with my girl' said Spike.

'Will she confirm that?' asked Sharon.

'I bloody well hope so!' said Spike 'otherwise I was having one hell of a wet dream!'

They all broke into laughter.

'What's the lucky girl's name and address?' asked Sharon.

'This week, it's Angie Dawson, next week who knows? And you can find her staying over at my place. Temporarily of course!' he said, searching his wallet for a business card.

'Are you ever serious?' asked Sharon.

'Only about sex!' he replied.

'And what about you . . . Dave? What were you doing at midnight last night?' asked Sharon.

Dave was in a dream. 'Ohh, umm, I had to go back into work, emergency, you know?'

'And what exactly do you do Dave?'

'I'm a manager at a Haulage firm, you know deliveries and exports. We had a late delivery coming in so had to be there.'

'A midnight delivery?' said Sharon.

'Well no . . . but I was there till after midnight, you know paperwork etc.'

'Paperwork etc? Couldn't it have waited till this morning to do that?'

'I like to keep things up together, you know, tight ship and all that.'

'What exactly was the shipment?'

'Uhmm . . . it was agricultural machine parts from France.'

'Heavy?'

'What?'

'The parts . . . they must be heavy?'

'Yeah, yeah tons, in crates you know?'

'Must have taken a while to unload then!'

'Yep, we worked hard for a couple of hours.'

'And who is we?' asked Bernie.

'Uhh . . . me and the driver unloaded it all, and then he had to drive back to France. Yeah it was hard work you know.'

'Why didn't you have a warehouseman there to unload it?'

'Oh no, it was a last minute delivery, you know, so I thought what the hell, I have to be there anyway so may as well do it myself . . . with the help of the driver.'

'What was his name?'

'Who . . . the driver? Ohh . . . Hans or something like that, I can't remember really.'

'Well I'm sure it'll be all in your paperwork, as you "run a tight ship" and all that. We'll be around in the morning to check it out, if that's alright by you?'

'You . . . your investigating a theft you say?' Dave asked nervously.

'Yeah that's right.' said Bernie.

'What exactly was uhhm, stolen?'

'I'm afraid we can't say at this stage sir' said Sharon 'we have to, "you know" keep it tight to our chest.'

Spike couldn't miss the pun. 'You can keep me tight to your chest anytime darlin!' he said, winking at Sharon and handing her one of his business cards. She looked at him and smiled, she did find him quite attractive.

Just at that moment Kev walked in. 'Hi guys, what's happened? You all look like you just lost a winning lottery ticket!'

Bernie referred to his notes and said, 'Are you . . . Kevin Mitchell?'

NINETEEN.

'Yeah, and who the fuck are you?' Kev retorted.

'They're Police!' Said Maggie.

'Oh, right . . . sorry then!'

'They're just investigating a theft in the area last night Kev, wasn't you was it?'

'Aww shit . . . I thought I'd gotten away with it . . . fair cop guv, you got me!' he said holding his arms out, wrists together.

'Okay, okay' said Bernie, 'enough of the amateur dramatics. Where were you at midnight last night?'

'Home in bed, asleep.'

'Anybody to confirm that?'

'Yep, my wife Lynn she was there too, snoring for England!'

'Okay Mr. Mitchell, we'll need to check with your wife.'

'Yeah fine, you can find her at "Billy's gym" off the high street, she's there doing her keep fit class until eight thirty. Tell her I'll be home in bed by ten.'

'Thanks, we will.' said Bernie.

'Now . . . where is Mr. Craig Warren?'

'He'll be here soon enough' said Danny, 'never misses his Friday night drink with the lads unless he has a late appointment.'

'And just what does Mr. Warren do for a living?' asked Sharon.

'He sells Insurance; you know . . . life policies and all that sort of stuff.'

'So he has late working hours and gets around a bit then?' said Sharon.

'Sometimes' said Danny, 'sometimes he has to work till eight or nine pm, and travel as well, no regular pattern!'

'Okay, well we will have to catch up with Mr. Warren tomorrow, we have other work to get on with now, and thank you all for your cooperation' said Bernie.

Just as they were going through the door, Bernie turned and said, 'See you in the morning about nine Mr Douglas, at the warehouse okay?'

'Yeah, suppose so' said Dave.

They went off to check out Kevin's alibi, then Bernie and Sharon headed back to base.

After they had gone, Dave ordered a large Brandy, and Danny joined him. They both knew this could be trouble, because Dave was not at the warehouse at all, he was collecting a delivery of cigarettes from his driver last night. Half of which he had just brought in for Danny; they were in his car which was parked around the side of the pub. He would normally have been at home before midnight, but the driver was late due to a hold up on the ferry crossing and was two hours late, so now Dave would have to go and sort some papers out, in order to cover his arse for last nights bogus delivery of machine parts.

'Bollocks, I could do without the "old bill" snooping around!' said Danny, 'perhaps we ought to calm down a bit on the old ciggy trading for a while Dave?'

'Nah, they're not after us, something else is keeping them busy. Don't worry, I'll go sort the papers out and it'll be fine. I better have another brandy before I go though!'

Dave left after downing his brandy, and Danny went through the back and met him at the side entrance and helped him bring the boxes inside.

'See ya later' Dave said.

Back in the bar, Maggie pulled Danny to one side.

'You're stupid Danny, you and Dave are going to get caught and we'll lose everything we got, why don't you just tell him that it has to stop. He'll soon find another mate to sell the gear on.

I just don't want us to lose this place Dan, I'm happy here!'

'Alright luv, I'll move this lot and tell him that I'm finished, okay?'

'It's for the best darlin, really' said Maggie, pecking him on the cheek.

Craig had just walked in, and of course Spike had to rib him somehow. 'Hey Craig! I'd do a runner if I were you mate, the old bill are looking for ya!'

'What?' he said turning around quickly and nervously looking around the pub.

'Gotcha!' said Spike almost falling off his bar stool laughing.

'Bastard!'

'Calm down mate!' said Kev 'he's only pulling your pisser again as usual.'

'Yeah, well sometimes it pisses me off . . . fucking about all the time!'

There was a communal 'oooooohh' from Spike, Danny and Kev.

'What's got in to you all of a sudden? Bad day at the office was it?' said Danny.

'Yeah, something like that!' said Craig managing a grin, 'Give us a pint then Dan.'

Danny pulled him a pint, and told him that the police really did want to talk to him. He turned a whiter shade of pale.

'Yeah, they want to ask you where you were at midnight last night, something about a theft or something' said Spike.

'Where are they now then?'

'Said they had other things to check out, and then left, perhaps they went round to your old folk's house to see you! Perhaps you should nip home and see eh?'

'No, I can't, I've got an appointment tonight' said Craig.

'Well, keep a lookout in your rearview mirror mate, they will probably have a tail on ya!' said Spike sniggering.

TWENTY.

8:30 pm, and back at the incident room, the team were assembled for the brief on the evenings operation. They were going to pick up the jogger from the park, should he show up.

If he were a true jogger in training, he probably had a routine training program and it was possible that he might use the same route every night.

The team wanted to bring him in to the station to ask a few questions if he appeared in the park tonight. If he didn't, it could be that he was the knifeman checking out the area. Dicky was hoping for a bit of a result to add to his one hospitalized witness.

At 9:00 pm, three male and three female detectives, were situated inside the park, posing as courting couples. They were to stroll around the perimeter at opposite sides to each other. Meanwhile, the rest of the squad were in position to cover all the exits. They all carried two way radios so that contact was ensured at all times.

If this guy was true to his training schedule, then he should enter the park around ten thirty. It was going to be a long wait for everybody.

Three miles away, Carol sat in her flat sipping vodka, contemplating her next move. She knew that the Police were snooping about, and maybe tonight she would have to suppress her need to go out and kill again. Last night's shambles would have to suffice her needs for now, until the heat died down a bit. It would not be long; the Police had nothing that would lead them to her. It was too late to drive over to meet her contact in Birmingham who fenced all her stolen gear. She still had some from her previous victim, but none from last night of course, so she decided to take the bag of clothes down to the launderette and put them through the washer/dryer ready for next time.

Back over in the park, the detectives were tired and agitated, awaiting the joggers' arrival. Then at ten twenty they were rewarded for their patience.

He entered the park through the very same gate as before, and as soon as he was in the cordon closed on him, there would be no escape for this guy! As he turned the bottom round of the park pathway, DC Keith Butler and DC Sophie Smith stood in front of him holding up their I.D. badges.

'Police!' said Keith, 'we would like to ask you a few questions sir if you don't mind?'

The jogger was clearly surprised, 'What's this all about?' he asked nervously.

'We're investigating an attack that happened here in the park last night. Can you tell us where you were last night sir?'

'Yeah, I got home from work, had a rest then went out for a run.'

'Where did you run to?'

'I ran round a few streets, then I came in here and did a lap, then I headed back home, why is there a law says I can't run at night?'

'No sir ... we just need to establish your whereabouts last evening that's all.'

'Well I've done nothing wrong, so if you don't mind I'll just carry on with my run tonight.'

He started to run off before Keith and Sophie could stop him. 'Hey . . . wait a minute we haven't finished yet!' said Sophie.

'Well I have, so go question some other fucker!' the jogger replied as he moved off into the distance.

Keith called on his radio, 'attention all teams . . . this is team two, jogger is on the move, and we need to apprehend to finish questioning! Over.'

'This is team one receiving . . . jogger is headed towards us, we will apprehend, over.'

The jogger was following the pathway around the perimeter of the park, and he was heading straight towards Sharon and Bernie, but he must have realized that they were also plain clothes police so he decided to cut across the cricket pitch back towards another gate.

'Fuck, here we go again!' said Bernie as he started to chase him across the pitch, slipping and sliding on the damp grass. A few seconds later he went headlong into a muddy patch and must have slid ten metres along on his front.

'Jeezus . . . look at my fucking suit!' he said angrily as he got up. There was mud and grassy stains all down his front. Sharon was pissing her pants laughing at the state of him.

The jogger had reached the gateway at the same time as team three did.

They apprehended him and read him his rights. 'What the fuck have I done?' the man demanded.

'We'll explain it all down at the station sir' said Duncan, taking a grip on his arm and leading him away.

WPC Elaine Carter spoke into her radio, 'This is team three reporting, subject apprehended, we are heading back to the vehicles, over.'

Out of the park and up a side street, the team three detectives and the detained jogger were getting into unmarked police car. The other teams boarded their unmarked police cars that were also parked there.

Meanwhile in the launderette alone and waiting for the dryer to finish, Carol was sitting partly obscured by the machines from the view through the window.

She moved back suddenly when she spotted a friend walking past the premises. '*Shit*' she thought, it would be a difficult situation should she be spotted down here doing her washing. Her friend in question would know that she always had her washing done for her usually. She moved quickly to the door to see where he had gone, but could not see him.

A minute later, the friend came out of the off-license next door carrying a small carrier bag; then he walked into the chip shop on the corner.

Carol decided to stay in the launderette until the coast was clear. She waited at her vantage point until she saw him coming out of the chippy, then quickly moved to the back of the shop taking cover behind a large drying machine.

Her friend was heading back towards the launderette with the carrier bag looped over his fingers, eating his chips as he walked along the sidewalk. He didn't even look up as he went past the window; he was too busy stuffing the chips in his mouth to worry about anything else around him.

The drying machine had finished, so Carol quickly bagged her clothes. She cautiously stepped outside, glanced up and down the street, then moved smartly into the doorway of her flat, key ready in hand to open the door and get inside before anyone had the chance to see her. Upstairs she sat again with a glass of vodka, she had nearly been rumbled by a passing friend.

She would have to be more careful in future.

TWENTY ONE.

Downtown at the nick, the jogger had been booked in as assisting in a line of enquiry, and was sitting in an interview room with DC Montgomery and WPC Carter, they had been the apprehending officers so therefore were given the task of interviewing the man. Firstly they reminded him that he had been brought into custody for failure to assist in their enquiries, it was purely a matter of procedure, he was not under arrest but it was urgent that he gave his assistance to further their enquiries.

'So I'm not under arrest then?'

'No sir, you are free to go, but first we would be very grateful if you would allow us to ask you some informal questions to clarify your whereabouts last evening.' said Duncan.

Standing up, the man said 'Well if I'm free to go, I'll leave now!'

'We still need to know where you were last night sir!'

'But you said I could go!'

'I did, but unless you are willing to answer a few simple questions, we will have to charge you with obstructing our enquiry, and at that stage you will be read your rights etc, entitled to a solicitor and everything takes twice as long . . . you could be here all night!'

'Okay, so I answer a few questions and I can go after yeah?'

'It's as simple as that sir.'

'Okay let's do this' the man said.

'Thank you sir we do appreciate it. You don't mind if I record our conversation do you?'

'Whatever.' He said with a shrug of his shoulders.

DCI Williams and DS Hayes were watching through a one way mirror at the side wall of the room, and listening in on the questioning.

Duncan started the tape recorder:

'Interview is commencing at eleven fifteen pm. Present are DC Montgomery and WPC Carter.

For the tape,' said Duncan looking directly at the jogger sat opposite him, 'would you please state your name, age and address.'

'I'm Jamie Butcher, 27 yrs old and live at 33, Windy-ridge Crescent, Cheltenham.'

'And do you live alone at that address Mr. Butcher?'

'No, I live there with my fiancée, Angela Lawson . . . Can you tell me what this is about please? Has Angela had an accident or something?' he asked worriedly.

'No, Mr. Butcher, this has nothing to do with your fiancée, but we cannot divulge anything about our investigation for the moment.'

'Okay. Mr. Butcher can you confirm that you are assisting us with our enquiries of your own free will, and have declined a representative at this moment.'

'Yeah that's correct. I've done nothing wrong, so lets just get on with this thing and I can get home to the shower, yeah?'

There was a moment's pause before the questions continued.

'Can you tell us where you were at midnight last night Mr. Butcher?' asked Duncan.

'I . . . was in bed by midnight, yep.'

'Was your fiancée also in bed?'

'Probably, but not with me!'

'You have just said that you live with your fiancée Mr Butcher?'

'That's right, but she's away on a training course, has been all week. She comes home tomorrow morning.'

'So you were home alone?'

'Yep, except for the cat.'

'Can you tell us what you were doing between six and midnight last night?'

'Uh . . . yeah, I got in from work around six. Fed the cat, then sat down with a meal from the microwave and watched the news on TV. Fell asleep on the sofa for a while. When I woke up I changed into my running gear, and then went for my run at about nine thirty. Got back in the house around eleven-ish.

Had a shower, a drink, then bed.'

'Is there anyone to confirm your whereabouts?'

'Don't think so, I didn't speak to anyone, I just put my iPod on, run my distance and then back to the house. The only people I saw were the ones I passed while I was out.'

'How often do you go running at night?'

'Well I do most of my training at night, because of work.'

'What are you training for?'

'Marathons, I run marathons, so have to put the mileage in you know, build up for each one. I'm currently in training for the New York marathon.'

'And how many have you run Mr. Butcher?'

'Fifteen' he said proudly.

'That's a lot of running,' said an impressed WPC Carter.

'Well it's what I'm good at.'

'Did you see or pass anyone near or in the park last night?'

'Umm . . . yeah, I passed a few people outside on the way round my route, then there was a couple as I passed by the pavilion in the park.'

'Were they the only people you saw in the park at that time?'

'Yeah . . . I noticed them because they looked a bit, I don't know, suspicious I suppose.'

'Tell us about the people you passed on the outskirts of the park then Mr. Butcher.'

'Umm . . . there was a young couple walking up towards Windyridge as I was coming up to the gate to enter the park.'

'Anyone else?' said Duncan.

'Umm . . . nope.' said Jamie. 'Oh, only some tart in her car doing her make up, parked at the end of our road when I got home, and that was all I think.'

Duncan turned to face the two way mirror where he knew the DCI would be watching, and gave a look that said everything he was thinking. *"Bingo."*

'Can you just run through that with us?' said Duncan.

'Yeah . . . but a cup of coffee would go down well right now!' said Jamie. 'Could do with some caffeine!'

'Okay, sure' said Duncan 'interview break at eleven twenty seven pm.' Then he switched the machine to standby. 'We'll get some coffee!'

He signaled to the WPC to follow him out of the room. This was a good time to check with Dicky to see what he had made of the interview so far. He was quite happy the way it was going, and excited about what Jamie Butcher had just said.

'This could be our biggest break yet' said Dicky, 'this person in the car could be our killer before she attacked Peter Sherman.

Let's just hope he got a good look at her!'

TWENTY TWO.

They took Jamie coffee. 'How much longer do you intend to keep me?' he asked.

'Not too long now sir.' said Duncan restarting the tape machine, 'Interview continuing at eleven thirty five pm. DC Montgomery, WPC Carter and Mr. Jamie Butcher present . . . so Jamie . . . tell us about the woman in the car.'

'Not much to tell really' he said, 'She had the interior light on and looked like she was doing her hair and make up in the rearview mirror as I went by.'

'Can you be more specific Jamie? Like the Colour of her hair, anything you can remember.'

'Okay, let me think . . . I ran by on the opposite side of the road, I don't think she even saw me because she was so sort of focused, on doing her hair, well it looked more like she was straightening a wig to me!'

'What colour was it Jamie?'

'I think red . . . yeah a red wig was what it looked like to me.'

'Anything else?' asked the WPC.

'Not as I ran by no, but I always stretch my legs out on the gate after I get back, you know, to stop them cramping up on me. So I was watching her while I did my cooling down and stretching. Well, after checking her hair and that, she turned the inside light off and sat there for a few minutes. Then she got out, locked the car and walked off in a direction towards the park. Then I went indoors, and like I said I . . .'

'Okay Jamie, just go back a little . . . can you tell us what she was wearing when you saw her step out of the car?'

'Umm . . . I think she had a denim jacket on, a very short dark skirt, possibly stockings and heeled shoes, and a kind of shoulder style handbag. I also remember thinking she was quite well built for a woman, you know, tall and quite broad really. I don't know, it was quite dark, but she definitely had the red hair though.'

'Okay . . . what about the car Jamie, any idea?'

'Oh yeah, it was a Vauxhall Vectra or an Astra, and it was dark blue or black maybe!'

'Are you sure it was a Vauxhall?'

'Yep, positive, because I got an Astra myself.'

'Any chance you got the Registration number of the woman's car?'

'Nah, sorry, I'm not really into the neighborhood watch thing! Can I go home now? I have to get up for work you know, and I'm knackered, it's been a long day.'

Duncan was consulting his notepad in which he had some prompts written down, 'Just a couple more questions Jamie . . . You say you went out for your run at . . . nine thirty pm approximately?'

'Yeah that's right.'

'Was the car there when you went out?'

'No . . . I would have seen it.'

'You say you got back to your house after the run at just before eleven pm, and that's when you first saw the car, correct?'

'That's right.'

'Did you see or hear it leave?'

'No, sorry.'

Another check of his notes, then he nodded at WPC Carter.

'Okay, terminating interview at eleven fifty.' she said, then turned it off and removed the tape.

Duncan said 'Just give us a few minutes Jamie, we just need to have a word with the guv'nor and see what we he says, okay?'

Jamie nodded then finished drinking the last drop of his cold coffee.

Outside the interview room Dicky was quite pleased with the outcome. Jamie Butcher seemed to be a genuine sort of guy, and he believed his story. He had also just described the clothing that Sharon Simmons and Bernie Webb had said the attacker was wearing, complete with wig. So unless he was trying to throw them off his scent by describing what he himself was wearing at the time of the attack, he had just confirmed the killers' clothing.

He had also given a time that the attacker was on the scene, and a vehicle sighting.

Dicky entered the interview room; he wanted a chat with Jamie Butcher before he let him go home.

'Mr. Butcher . . . I'm Detective Chief Inspector Williams. Thank you for your cooperation this evening. We are investigating an assault that took place close to your home, and it's quite possible that you passed the attacker, that's why we brought you in. However, we need to confirm your movements last night, and in order to verify that, we have one more thing we need to do in order to eliminate you from our enquiries.

I'm going to let you go home now, but feel it necessary to send an escort with you, and I'd like to check your house over if you don't mind?'

'But why? I've helped you haven't I, why do you need to check out my house god dammit!' Jamie said angrily. 'That's bloody typical, I've a good mind to call a lawyer, and make you guys go through all the proper procedures!'

'That's your prerogative Mr. Butcher, but if you do, we will have to hold you here in custody while you get hold of a brief, then we file to get a search warrant allowing us to search your premises. Anyway it's your choice. You can continue helping as you have done and we will be all done in a couple of hours, or we can probably drag it out a couple of days.'

'You fucking cops are all the same, always pushing the public that bit too much, all take and no give! Well as I said before, I have nothing to hide so I would be grateful if you let me go now. Its fine, search the place, you won't find anything!'

'Okay Mr. Butcher' said Dicky, 'and despite what you think, we are very grateful to you tonight. You have given us some vital evidence. I'll see to it that my men work as quickly as permissible, and then we can leave you in peace!'

With that, Dicky detailed DC Mclean and DS Clark along with two uniformed police officers, the task of searching Jamie Butchers house.

It was nearly three am before they left his home, having found nothing in the house or his car to link him to the attacks. They also saw where he had claimed the car was parked at the end of the road. It would be about a five minute walk at least to the park from there.

Tim and Alan thanked him and left along with the other two uniformed officers.

TWENTY THREE.

It was Saturday 9:30 am.

'Good morning Mr. Douglas!' Said Sharon loudly, as she and Bernie stood in the doorway of Dave Douglas' office at the haulage yard. 'How are you this morning?'

'Shit!' said Dave, 'do you always creep up on people like that? Nearly gave me a heart attack!'

'Oh we wouldn't want that now would we?' said Bernie, 'Well not before you show us the paperwork for Thursday night's delivery anyway! I expect you have it handy, ready for us to see don't you?' he said sarcastically.

'Yep, here it is all ready for you, I know you are busy people so I got it ready as soon as I got in this morning,' said Dave trying to sound as cooperative as possible.

'Really?' Sharon said as she took the paperwork from him.

She held two pieces of headed photocopied A4 paper in front of her. It itemized the details of a shipment of machine parts from France.

Eight boxes in all. Time and date of delivery. Signature boxes for the delivery driver and the acceptor of the delivery at the bottom.

'I'm guessing these are yours and the driver's signatures?' she said, as she was pointing at the scribble in the boxes at the bottom of the second page.

'Yes ma'am' he said.

Bernie had a look, 'funny . . . they both look very similar in the strokes to me, but there again I'm no handwriting expert!' he said while looking at Dave. 'I can't make out the drivers scribble, what was his name again?'

'I think it was . . . Franz' said Dave.

'But I thought you said it was Hans when we spoke to you yesterday?' said Sharon.

Dave had coloured up now, but trying hard not to show his guilt, he said 'Hans, Franz all sounds the bloody same to me. Bloody French names!' tutting and flicking his eyes upward.

'Okay Mr. Douglas, the paperwork appears to be in order.' said Bernie.

'Good. That's great!' said Dave with a smile and a sigh of relief.

'We just need to see the boxes now!' said Sharon, giving him one of her "gotcha" smiles.

'The bu, bu, boxes?' he stammered.

'Yeah, you know, the ones listed here as containing the agricultural machinery parts!' she said, 'We will need to see them . . . is there a problem?'

'No, no problem,' said Dave.

'So shall we . . . ? Over there are they?' asked Sharon, pointing towards the warehouse across the yard from the office.

Dave although shocked at the request, had prepared the sheets carefully to show the numbers of boxes already in the warehouse. So when they went out to check them, they did tally with the identification numbers on the invoice. He had simply duplicated a shipment delivery invoice from the previous week, onto headed paper. He then photocopied them after adding a forged signature of the driver, along side his own. Unless they took it further and checked out the driver he would be in the clear. It was a chance he had to take.

Walking back to the office after the checks, Bernie asked Dave which car was his, pointing towards three cars parked in a row.

'The blue Ford Estate car . . . why?'

'Nothing to be concerned about at the moment' said Bernie sternly, 'and . . . thank you Mr. Douglas, let's hope we don't have a need to bother you again, eh?'

It was a simple warning to stay in line.

'Oh . . . sure thing' he replied.

Sharon and Bernie were then on their way to pay a visit to see Craig Warren at his parents house.

Meanwhile DCI Williams and DS Hayes were at the hospital waiting to interview Peter Sherman. He was sitting up and able to talk this morning, but still very weak. Doctors were just doing the rounds, and then they would be allowed in to see him.

Peter Sherman was a poorly man. He had been lucky not to have any vital organs permanently damaged during the attack on Thursday night.

The surgeons had repaired his slashed leg, made good the damage to his large intestine and removed his spleen. He had lost a lot of blood and had to have several transfusions during the op.

The detectives were only able to take a partial statement from Peter Sherman, but he revealed some positive information for the team. The doctors had intervened on the interview, when they could see that Peter was becoming too exhausted. The interview would have to resume later, after he had more rest.

Dicky wanted to get back to the station as soon as they had finished with Peter, to add the detail to the attacker's profile, which was now beginning to take shape.

DS Clark and DC Mclean had paid a visit to Jeff Markham's address. A neighbour said that he had gone to work early but finished at lunchtime on a Saturday, and that he would probably go to the "Westchester" for a pint straight after work.

Tim and Mac decided that they would go there to see him later. Meanwhile they would take a trip to "Cleo's club" to speak to the doorman, Stuart Wiggins.

At the club they found the door open, and a gaggle of cleaners gabbling noisily while they mopped beer stained floors, and cleared the tables which were strewn with glasses and cigarette butts in ashtrays. They were in luck; "their man" was changing barrels of beer and restocking the shelves when they arrived.

'Stuart Wiggins?' asked Mac.

'Who wants to know?' said the very large coloured gentleman hefting a barrel in each hand.

'I am DC Mclean and this is DS Clark.'

Stuart set down the barrels, 'Look' he said,

'Whatever that long haired punk says, I didn't stick his head down the bog, alright!'

'Tell us more' said Tim with a smile.

'That's what you come here for right? He reported me to you guys?'

'Who?' said Mac, enjoying seeing the guy squirm.

Stuart realized the police were here for something else. 'Only joking!' He said, trying to look cool. 'So what's up?'

'Were you working here on Thursday evening?'

'Yep, I was here from about seven pm till after two am when we kicked out. You know, emptied the club.'

'Do you know many of the customers?' asked Tim.

'Well yeah, quite a few of the regular ones anyway.'

'Do you remember seeing four lads who claim to have been in on Thursday? They say they are regulars. Their names are Steve Langdon, Jeff Markham, Mike Mason and Ashley Corbett.'

'Yeah, yeah I saw the guys on Thursday night, they came in about nine thirty-ish. I was working the inside of the club at the time. Then at ten thirty I go to work the entrance door till closing time.'

'So you would have seen them leaving then?' Said Tim.

'Yeah, they went out with a few others around about two am. Oh yeah . . . but Jeff left earlier round about ten forty five.'

'Was he with anyone else?'

'Not that I noticed really, I was dealing with what you might call an awkward customer at the time, so

I didn't really take a lot of notice. Generally the four guys come and go together though!'

'Okay, thanks Mr. Wiggins, you've been a great help!'

Tim and Mac knew they really needed to speak to Mr Jeff Markham urgently now!

TWENTY FOUR.

Bernie Webb and Sharon Simmons arrived at Craig Warren's parents' home to find him cleaning the inside of his car with a vacuum cleaner. It was parked on the drive in front of the garage.

'Craig Warren?' Bernie asked, as he walked up behind the man.

'That's me . . . and you are, oh let me guess . . . ummm, the police!' he said turning and pointing the nozzle at Bernie.

'Full marks!' said Sharon, 'you have obviously been talking to your mates down at "The Empty Jug" . . . I am DC Simmons and this is my colleague DC Webb . . . your car dirty is it?'

He turned off the vacuum. 'Well I'm not cleaning the dirt off the driveway am I? What do you want?'

'We are investigating an assault which was committed in the area on Thursday night. Can you tell us where you were around midnight on Thursday Mr. Warren?'

'I heard it was a theft!' he said in a cocky manner.

Sharon was quick to rectify her slip of the tongue. 'Correct . . . it was a theft following an assault! Now, you were where on Thursday night?'

'I had an appointment in Worcester.'

'What time was that?'

'Eight pm.'

'And, what time did you arrive home?'

'About eleven pm.'

'Anyone to confirm that?'

'Yeah, mum was still up. In fact she made me a cup of tea when I got in.'

'That's a long time for an appointment?'

'Yeah well I stopped off for a drink on the way back.'

'So do you live here with your parents?'

'Duh . . . yeah, well half of them anyway!' he said in a sullen sort of way.

'Are your parents split then?' asked Sharon, trying to show some concern.

'No, but may as well be! Dad has Alzheimer's, don't even know who we are some days.'

'I'm sorry Mr. Warren we didn't know. As sad as that is, we will need to check your alibi with your mother. Is she home?'

'Yep, follow me, just remember she's under a lot of stress looking after dad, so go easy okay?'

'We will Mr. Warren, don't worry.'

Inside Mrs. Warren was helping her husband with his breakfast. He was in an unpleasant mood!

'Who the fuck are you? Leave me alone, I don't want to go out!' he shouted at them.

'Arthur, that's no way to speak to Craig's friends now is it?'

'They're not my friends mum, they're the police! They want you to confirm that I was here at eleven pm last Thursday night!'

'Okay Mr. Warren! We would like to talk to your mother alone please.' Interrupted Bernie. 'Mrs. Warren, we understand your situation here, but can we have a word in private please?'

She looked towards her son, as if asking for permission.

'Go on' he said, looking at the detectives, 'I'll finish with dad . . . and hey, remember what I said about going easy!'

They went into the lounge, sitting in a semi circle around the coffee table.

'Mrs. Warren . . . can you remember what time your son came home on Thursday evening?'

'Why?'

'Oh yes, sorry, we are investigating an assault that occurred nearby, and we are making some general enquiries that's all.'

'He came home at eleven pm and I made him a cup of tea.' she said, in a rehearsed parrot fashion. Then she offered 'He didn't do it!'

'We didn't say he has done anything Mrs. Warren, we are just making enquiries so that we can eliminate him from our list, that's all. Are you okay? You look upset?'

'I'm fine, now will you go please? I have to look after my husband!'

'Yes of course, and thank you for your time.'

As they stood up to leave, Sharon glanced across the room at the sideboard, which she noticed was full of framed photos.

'May I take a look?' she asked, pointing across the room at the photos.

Silvia Warren nodded a yes in reply. Sharon's eyes danced from one to the other. All the photos were of a pretty girl, the ages appeared to range from around two, up to late teens.

'Who's the girl in these photos?'

'My lovely daughter' she said, tears welling in her eyes.

'She's very pretty.' Sharon said, picking up one in a frame. 'Where is she now? Married?'

'No she's dead!'

'Sorry?' Sharon was not sure what she heard her say.

'I said she's dead. Nearly six years now!'

'I'm very sorry . . . we're very sorry.' said Sharon slightly embarrassed.

'Now you must go, I have things to get done!' said Mrs Warren, suddenly feistier, snatching the photo from Sharon and cradling it to her chest as if to protect it.

They were shown out by Craig. 'Happy now that you have upset my family?'

'Sorry Mr. Warren, we are only trying to do our job. Goodbye.' said Bernie.

As they walked back down the drive Sharon let out a 'Phew! That was a bit intense wasn't it? An angry son with a sick dad and a sad mother, Jesus!'

'Yeah you're right there Shaz, but I think there was something else that they weren't telling. Maybe we should keep a bit of an eye on Craig Warren!'

Bernie and Sharon were heading back to the station now to report in on their interview findings.

Meanwhile, Tim and Mac were on their way back to "The Westchester", to await Jeff Markham's entrance.

At the station the other detectives were piecing together evidence, while Dicky and Alan were listing the latest developments from their interview with Peter Sherman, along with the information coming in from the other detectives. They were told that they could return to finish the interview after Peter had had a few hours rest, so they planned to return later that evening.

Dicky had sent out some uniformed officers, to do a door to door check of the neighborhood of "the jogger" Jamie Butcher. It was quite possible that someone else had seen the attacker or the car around the area on Thursday evening.

'So far so good' Alan said to nobody in particular, as he wrote another vital clue up on the white board. 'now we're beginning to get somewhere.'

TWENTY FIVE.

Craig Warren was in the kitchen of his parents' house drinking tea. His mother entered looking worried. She need not have, she had told the story exactly as instructed by her son.

'Well done mum, you were cool, they didn't suspect anything so don't worry. Here take this pot of tea in for you and dad, I'll be in shortly.' He handed her the tray, but she started to cry.

'Why did those police come here? If you're only out helping those young homeless girls on the street, why did they come here thinking you've assaulted somebody?'

'Look, don't worry mum I haven't done anything wrong, we know we're doing the right thing, the police are just checking something else out, and it's nothing to do with our good work! Go on now, take the tea in for dad.'

Since the murder of his twin sister, Craig Warren had sworn at her graveside that he would take revenge for her, and he would do this by eliminating the scum who used and abused prostitutes. He would dispatch them in the manner that his sister had suffered. But as far as his mother was concerned, the story he told her was that he was helping young girls on the streets, the ones who were homeless and had fallen into the addiction of drugs, financed by prostitution.

In the earlier years, Craig and his sister had frequent rows with their father, who back then, had the first stages of Alzheimer's, but they didn't know it then. He had become nasty and argumentative, especially with Carol; she seemed to aggravate his condition without knowing it. She eventually left home, but then fell into the trap of the homeless and drug community on the streets; she also sold herself to pay for it.

Craig had kept in contact with her, but could not persuade her to return home. He helped her as best as he could financially, but the drug habit was becoming more demanding and taking over her life.

Only nine months after leaving home, the family were informed of her death. She had died at the hands of a crazed knifeman. Craig was distraught following her death and was committed to a mental institution, where he spent two and a half years undergoing psychiatric therapy. The therapy calmed him, but didn't cure him, and he spent his time planning how he would avenge his twin sister when he eventually got released.

It was after his release from hospital that they decided to move from the outskirts of London, to the town of Cheltenham Spa in the Cotswold's, and that was 3 years ago.

Craig's mother didn't want to stay around the area where she had lost her daughter, also his father now had full blown Alzheimer's, and apart from needing a smaller house, the money left over would help them to live decently until Craig found work.

It took six months before he got the job with the insurance company, not good money but he got extra bonuses now and again with a good policy sale. This was partly the reason he was robbing his victims as well as killing them, the extra money helped out at home.

Of course, his fiancée Sarah was totally unaware of Craig's alias, Carol, and even more, the lies to his mother regarding the support of homeless girls.

He and Sarah frequently rowed about the fact that she wanted to live with him in their own place, but could not seem to afford to. She knew about his evening appointments with clients, which were true, and that he would earn good bonuses for a signing, what she could not accept, was that no extra money was going into their shared bank account which they had set up to finance the purchase of their own home.

The police snooping around didn't bother Craig; he believed he was far cleverer than they were. He would now set a date for his next victim. Meanwhile he did need a trip to see his "fence" who resided in Birmingham, so that he could clear his stash out of the flat, that should bring him in a couple of hundred pounds. He punched the number into his mobile and spoke to his contact, saying that he would drive up there Monday evening after his last appointment of the day.

TWENTY SIX.

The bar at "The Westchester" was pretty quiet when Tim and Mac arrived. They each had a coke and went to sit at a table which was by the door.

Here they had a vantage point of who came in, and be able to block a getaway should it be necessary.

At 12:15 pm Mike Mason walked in with whom they assumed to be Jeff Markham. They walked straight to the bar, not spotting Tim and Mac sat to the one side. The detectives approached them and asked the question as they stood directly behind them.

'Jeff Markham?'

As they both turned together Mike said, 'Oh yeah, Jeff, these are the "old bill" that were wanting to talk to you the other day.'

'I'm DS Clark and this is DC Mclean, can we have a word?'

'Sure, why not!' he said cockily, taking a large swallow of beer.

'So Mr. Markham, can you tell us where you were last Thursday evening from say seven pm onwards?'

'Yeah, I met the guys in here for a beer or two before going to "Cleo's club".'

'When you say the guys, you're talking about Mike here, Steve Langdon and Ashley Corbett, yeah?'

'Yep that's right.'

'And were you in the club all night?'

'Uhh . . . yep.'

'You sure about that, because the doorman says you left around about ten forty five?'

There was a slight pause before he answered. 'Right yeah, I remember, I wasn't feeling too good so I went home early, one too many glasses of sherry I think.'

His pal Mike's reaction gave the game away, he nearly choked on his beer. Tim knew he was lying to them.

'Can anyone verify that sir?' asked Tim.

'Yeah Mike here.' he said without a pause.

Mike said 'Well . . . all I know is, he had a fucking big lump in his trousers when he left, so he must have gone home to be sick over his girlfriend!' then he burst out laughing.

Tim looked at Mac and raised an eyebrow. 'Okay, funny, but let's cut the crap shall we? Now either you can answer our questions here, or we can take a trip down the station and maybe you will get home some time tomorrow! So what do you think?'

'Okay okay, so I left a bit early, so what's the big deal?'

'We're investigating a serious assault which happened not far from here, so where were you at midnight Thursday?'

'I can't seem to remember!'

Just then the other two lads Steve and Ashley came in.

Ashley looked at the two policemen saying, 'what the fuck do you want again? Why don't you just piss off outta here and leave us to have a drink in peace!' He was very agitated as though he was high on something.

He came towards Tim aggressively; Tim stood his ground until they were stood virtually nose to nose. Then without any hesitation, Ashley head butted Tim sending him crashing backwards into a table. Blood was splattered over his face and was running freely from his broken nose as he sat on the floor cupping his face in his hands and groaning in pain.

Before Tim had hit the floor, Mac had launched himself at Ashley Corbett. He caught him in the midsection and drove him backwards into the bar knocking the wind from his lungs, he followed up with a sharp punch to the solar plexus causing Ashley to double up, then a twist of his arm around his back, and the man was on the floor with Mac sitting on top of him snapping on a set of restraints. He was going nowhere, but his mates Mike and Jeff were already on their way out of the door. The guy named Steve just stepped backwards out of the way; he didn't seem to want to get involved.

Mac didn't bother to try and catch up with them; he knew they would be picked up later. At the moment he needed to get Tim to hospital and Ashley Corbett to the cells for assaulting an officer.

Mac called the station on his mobile, for a van to take in Ashley Corbett and Steve Langdon while he took Tim for treatment. He also quickly informed DCI Williams of the incident, who sent out two patrol cars to pick up Jeff Markham and Mike Mason to bring them in for questioning.

It was a couple of hours later that Mac and Tim, "the walking wounded", arrived back at the station. Tim had a splint strapped to the length of his nose by tape, and what was the start of two lovely black eyes. The piss-take comments were to be expected from the guys.

'Hey up, Tim's had a fight with his misses again!' came from Sharon, and,

'That'll teach you to spy through keyholes!' from Barney Miller.

Dicky Williams had a grin as wide as the Severn estuary, 'Shit, I hope the collar was worth it Tim!' he said.

Tim was trying to put on a brave face but had a splitting headache; he walked straight through to the water dispenser at the far end of the room, and poured himself a cup of ice cold water to wash down the painkillers he had just taken out of his pocket.

After swallowing them down he turned and said, 'Well thanks for the concern guys, its nice to know who your friends are anyway?'

After the piss taking had died down Dicky said 'Seriously though, are you alright Tim?'

'I'll survive, it'll take more than some dirt bag like Corbett to stop me on this case!'

'Okay then, listen up guys, we have evidence from the horse's mouth as it were.

Peter Sherman wouldn't swear on it, but during his own attack, he and this fucker were face to face in the struggle and he said after thinking it through, that he was pretty sure that it could have been a man. He said the attacker was strong, well built and had short black hair under the wig . . . I'll pick up my winnings later' said Dicky with a smile.

A trickle of chatter filled the room. 'I said it was' said one. 'I fucking knew it!' said another, and so on until Dicky spoke again.

'Okay, so what else have we turned up in the last twenty four hours?'

'Mac, looks like you and Tim have had some action, do you want to fill us in?'

Tim sat quietly while Mac did the honors describing the events that happened from the first confrontation with the small gang from "The Westchester", right up to two hours ago.

'So do you think that one of them may be our serial killer Mac?' asked Duncan.

'Well we can't rule out Jeff Markham, because we haven't spoken to him properly yet, and he is of similar build to our attacker, but the other three don't really fit the profile or descriptions we have so far. We think they're just a bunch of thugs. Other than that we will need to charge Ashley Corbett with assaulting a police officer, Tim here. But mainly we need to find out why Jeff Markham did a runner, he must have something to hide, and he did leave his mates in the nightclub at around ten forty five on that Thursday night.'

'We'll do that alright' said Alan Hayes writing Jeff Markham's` name up on the board as a possibility.

'How did you and Sharon get on with Mr. Douglas at the warehouse Bernie?'

'Ah yes our Mr. Douglas, what a very cooperative man he is, in fact far too efficient and cooperative. He doesn't seem to fit our killer spec, but again something is going on over there that we will need to check out. Sharon and I will try to slot in a little surveillance on him where we can. Okay with that guv?'

'Okay, only nailing our killer is top priority at the moment, but yeah if you think he's up to something naughty, then check him out!'

'Of course guv ; our other man, Craig Warren, now he would fit the profile but has an alibi for last Thursday, his mother . . .

The problem is, she seemed under duress from her son, she spoke word for word what he had told us, almost rehearsed it seemed. She was also nervous and upset. Sharon picked up a photo of her daughter whom we found out had died six years earlier, it seems a long time to still be grieving that badly, in fact I don't think it was grief so much as anger.

We have nothing on him at the moment but we think he needs to be watched. One other thing, his car is a white Volkswagen Golf, he was cleaning it when we arrived.'

'Right, thanks guys, keep up the good work, we are making some progress . . . Alan, put Craig Warren on that shortlist as a possible suspect! Then we'll go back over to the hospital and see if Peter Sherman has any more information for us.'

TWENTY SEVEN.

Saturday evening Craig and Sarah were in the "Jug" with their friends, they were sat around two tables near the back of the bar.

There was the usual banter around the table, except Craig was not really in the "banter" mood tonight, he would rather go out and take another victim, but he knew that he couldn't, he had to try and control his personal vendetta.

Sarah said, 'what's up with you tonight Craig? You've been bloody moody since we came out tonight, cheer up for Christ's sake!'

'Yeah cheer up you miserable fucker, and get a round in' said Kev swilling back the last of his pint.

'Okay okay, sorry guys it's just that dad hasn't been too good today, you know, and it's taking its toll on mum and me, but we'll cope. Same again everyone?'

He got up and went to the bar, smiling to himself because he knew that he could fool his best mates and even his fiancée.

The others of course, because they didn't know his true background, all felt a little guilty after he had told them about his dad.

When Craig returned with the drinks Dave was bragging about how he had fooled the police with the machine parts.

'No . . . they won't be back, I was too convincing. You know I should get an "Oscar" for my performance this morning, oh . . . cheers Craig.'

'Well I wouldn't get too cocky mate, the police can turn up anytime, so be careful!' Spike warned, 'mind you, that one detective was quite attractive.'

'Nah, he wasn't my kind of guy' joked Kev.

'Not the guy you plonker, the bird.' Spike replied seriously, and then realized the joke was on him for a change.

Danny called Dave to one side, 'Listen mate, do we have a delivery next week?'

'Yeah, I should get a call perhaps Monday for a load coming in on Thursday night, why?'

'It's just that Maggie is getting twitchy, she wants me to stop having the ciggy's off you, says it's too risky.'

'Nah don't worry, that thing with the cops snooping around was nothing to do with our scam, and they won't be checking me again, as I said, I had them eating out of my hand.'

'I'm not worried, it's just that we will have to do it behind Maggie's back from now on. So we're on for Thursday then yeah?' said Dan.

'Should be, I'll tip you the wink as soon as I know okay mate? Right then it's my round!'

Craig sat in sufferance for the best part of the evening, drinking and listening to the others telling their stupid jokes, and watching their childish behavior. He knew that he couldn't stomach this for much longer; he had to get out of there.

He turned to Sarah, 'Hey babe, I'm a bit worried about mum coping with dad so I think we better get going!'

'No, she'll be okay luv, don't worry.' Sarah said, 'she's quite used to dealing with your dad now, have another drink.'

Craig's anger reached boiling point, and he blew.

'Well fuck you, you selfish bitch!' he said angrily rising from his seat.

Sarah was shocked at his outburst, and just sat there mouth open looking at him.

His friends were also surprised by the way Craig had "lost it" momentarily, and before any of them could console him, he was already storming out of the door.

Just across the street in an unmarked police vehicle, DC Keith Butler and DC Sophie Smith were on surveillance duty, monitoring Craig Warren's movements.

Assignments had been switched in case officers were recognized from previous interviews. They had been slumped in the front seats of the car for hours, since Craig and his fiancée had entered the bar earlier. They knew it would be a long night, but they both sat bolt upright, as they realized it was Craig who had come flying out through the door of the pub.

'Shit!' said Keith, 'It's him, come on we'll follow on foot, he may just be heading home.'

They exited the car and calmly crossed the road, by which time Craig had disappeared around the corner. They soon had him in view but allowed him to gain distance in front, they didn't want to spook him or give the game away, and sure enough, he walked directly home. They decided to just observe from the end of the road, which was about 50 metres from the house. The time was eleven pm, and they had been stood across the road from the house for forty minutes now.

Keith said 'Sod this Soph, I'm going to get the car and bring it round, I'm absolutely knackered.'

'Okay, you go and get it you poor old fart. I'll just step over here behind this hedge until you come back.'

Inside the house, Craig had been upstairs watching Sophie from behind a gap in the closed curtains of his darkened bedroom window. He had spotted them outside the pub when he came out, and saw them trailing him when he had a half glance behind as he turned into his road.

He had a wicked grin on his face. '*So, the police are tailing me*' he thought, '*maybe we can have some fun!*'

Two minutes later, Keith pulled up by the curb and Sophie got in. They drove passed the house slowly, seeing that there were no lights on in the house.

'Perhaps they're in the back room' said Sophie, 'we wouldn't be able to see the light from the road.'

Keith turned the car at the end of the road, and just as they were making another slow pass, Craig Warren came out of the front door. Keith had to keep going otherwise they would have been spotted, so he carried on past and turned left back towards the pub.

Craig quickly got into his car and drove off in the opposite direction, but he held back until he saw the lights of the unmarked police car coming back around the corner at the other end of the road. When he was sure they had spotted him, he accelerated away, turning left then right and back out onto the Lansdowne road, basically he drove around in a circle and back to the house and parked up.

Back inside, he waited and watched from his vantage point up in his bedroom window.

Keith drove around for about twenty minutes but could not work out where Warren had gone.

'Just a thought Keith' said Sophie, 'do you think he spotted us, because if he did, he could be taking the piss couldn't he?'

'Nah, no way did he catch on we were watching him,' Keith said confidently.

'Well do me a favour eh . . . just drive around past his house again will you?'

As they turned into Craig Warrens' road, Keith was about to say 'I told you so,' when he saw Craig's car parked on the drive in front of the garage door.

'Bollocks! You were right Soph, he is taking the piss!'

As they drove by, Craig was stood looking out of his bedroom window with the light on, he gave a little knowing wave to them as they drove slowly past, and then he drew the curtains closed again.

'Oh fuck it!' said Keith.

TWENTY EIGHT.

Jeff Markham and Mike Mason were picked up early Sunday Morning from their homes, a little shocked by the knocks on their doors at 6:00 am.

After interviews and holding them both for five hours, they were both released. There was nothing to hold them for, apart maybe for leaving the scene of the fracas at "The Westchester", when Ashley Corbett head butted Tim.

Mike Mason had his alibi from the doorman at "Cleo`s club", and Jeff Markham's current girlfriend said he left the club then stayed at her place the rest of the night.

Tim and Mac had conducted the interviews, and after discussion with DCI Williams they released the two thugs, although not totally convinced of Markham's story.

When he was far enough away from the police station, Jeff Markham sent a text to two people from the contacts list in his mobile phone, they were only labeled as **"B"** and **"M"**, the message read; **"Had run**

in with cops. Not a prob. Need to stay clear for while. Spk soon. J".

Both recipients understood the message when they received it, and for the need to play it safe.

Unknown to the police, Jeff Markham had been a drug dealer for the past eighteen months, and part of a small local syndicate dealing in "coke baggies". Cocaine which is mixed with baking powder, then bagged up in small self seal bags. They distribute these drugs in clubs and pubs throughout the city, but they're smart and know how to deal discreetly.

Jeff's day job as a plasterer is the ideal cover for his "other work". He's never used the drugs himself, he simply preys on the weak ones that need it, and they're mainly young teenagers who he makes lots of money from.

He had left the club early on that Thursday night because he had a meeting with the syndicate members. There was a new shipment coming in within the next few days and the gang needed to finalize the details of the pick-up.

There are three main players in the syndicate and Jeff Markham is one of them, all planning and distribution decisions are made by the three, nothing moves unless it is 100% safe. When in contact with each other by phone, they only use the first letter of their first name.

The gang of three are Jeff Markham, known as "J", Robert (Bob) Morgan known as "B", who runs a local landscape gardening business, and Mark Wainright, known as "M", who is a partner in an engineering company based in Tewkesbury. None of them has any sort of police record, and that's how they intend to keep it.

The meetings and distribution of the "gear", always takes place at the home of "B" the second man of the syndicate; he owns a large house in secured grounds, over in Down Hatherley, on the outskirts of Cheltenham.

Here, his CCTV ensures the privacy required for their money spinning work, and their planning meetings. Morgan puts up most of the money.

Mark Wainright has the contacts abroad; he coordinates the shipments and deliveries into the country. He also arranges the "mixing and bagging" of the "coke".

Jeff Markham is the main distributer, often managing to clear a shipment on his own, that way he can make more money for himself. Sometimes he'll recruit a "user" to help distribute it, the payment being a few free "coke baggies".

TWENTY NINE.

It was mid afternoon on Sunday, when DCI Williams and DS Hayes returned from visiting Peter Sherman at the hospital. He was recovering pretty well now and was able to give a full statement to the detectives.

The killers' profile was building nicely, and Dicky and Alan were just about to add the latest description and detail they had gleaned from Peter Sherman.

'Okay Al, let's see what we can add to the MO chart' said Dicky.

1) The killer.

- ❖ Dresses like a female prostitute.(but may be male).
- ❖ Red or Blonde wig.
- ❖ Semi high heels.
- ❖ Short skirts and panty hose/stockings.
- ❖ Cheap costume jewellery.
- ❖ Heavy on the make up.
- ❖ Drives a dark Vauxhall Astra or Vectra car?

- ❖ Weapon—Knife, possibly a surgeon's scalpel?
- ❖ Attacks usually late evening Friday or Thursday?
- ❖ Theft of possessions. (Not mobiles)?
- ❖ Caucasian.
- ❖ 190lbs (13st-6lbs) approx.
- ❖ Size 9 shoes.
- ❖ Short dark hair.
- ❖ Right handed.
- ❖ Has a duty to kill?

'Weapon—Witness—Motive, the three things that would generally lead to a suspect, we need to explore the questions here!' Said Dicky.

'We have a witness, and we know what the weapon is but do not have it. We don't know what the motive is. ***"You are destined to die tonight" "You must die tonight"*** The attacker spoke these words, Alan, so he must have a reason for saying it!'

'He's angry.'

'He has a duty to kill?'

'Uses a surgeon's scalpel.'

'Dresses up like a prostitute . . . but what is the link here?'

Alan was deep into analysis. 'He's obviously using the prostitute disguise to hide behind, so is he afraid of being recognized or is there a reason to dress like that? Perhaps he's a scorned cross dresser? Is the disguise to make him inconspicuous?

He says that the victim must die . . . so he has some sort of purpose or reason why, and he's using the same method, the abdominal slice and the carotid for the "coup de gras".

It could be ritualistic? Copycat killing or revengeful? The thefts of personal items are possibly just part of the show, he's not killing just for the prize of the possessions, it's definitely more than that.'

'I think your right Al, this isn't about theft of possessions, and I don't believe its ritual either, otherwise he would probably leave some sort of mark on the victim, like a cross or symbol of some kind, like a pentagon for instance, don't you agree?' said Dicky.

Alan was nodding in agreement. 'Possibly.'

'So copycat or revenge, or even both! But this is still supposition, we have nothing concrete as yet!'

'So, let's put out the description we have from Peter Sherman to all mobile units and uniformed officers on foot. Then I think we need to concentrate on finding the car, so let's put the effort into trolling through the CCTV tapes that we have gathered, and see if we can spot the killer or the car.

Equally as important is to check out past cases using a similar MO as this, I know that some work has been done on this already, but we may need to go further back in time and further afield. Finally, if we can try to trace the stolen items, we can get to our attacker from that angle, find the fence and we may get a name.'

'Oh yes, can someone check out the background on these two?' He said tapping his finger on the flip chart next to the names of Craig Warren and Jeff Markham. 'They seem to be the only possible suspects that we have in the frame at the moment, let's pay them a visit and ask for voluntary samples for DNA testing, see if they have any objections, and let's clarify our suspicions, okay.'

The detectives who were present took on the tasks without being directed by their boss, they knew what they had to do, so got on with it.

Alan asked Dicky 'What's your personal gut feel on this?'

Dicky curled his lip and shrugged, 'Not sure, but could be he has been hurt mentally by someone, and thinks that by killing same types that he has taken his revenge in some way? Or maybe someone he loves has been hurt or attacked in a similar way, and again he feels he must avenge them.'

'If we look at his MO, the first victim was cut across the abdomen and the carotid artery, but it was a bit messy. There was more than one cut at the abdomen, and the cut to the carotid artery went from ear to ear! That suggests to me that he's not a surgeon, so I believe that the scalpel thing is not a link.

The following victims had much cleaner cuts, one to the abdomen and one short cut right on the artery. This tells us that he became more skilled with each kill. He is executing them with accuracy and purpose now. It could possibly be to do with the element of surprise, where the victim doesn't have time to react to what is going on . . . but when we get to Peter Sherman, he faces resistance and has to improvise and that is where he slips up.

Again its messy, he gets involved in a fight then loses an earring, which we find with a little blood on, which could give us his DNA, but the blood could belong to the "vic".

That reminds me, I haven't heard from the labs yet whether they have enough blood to compare against our register; we need to chase that;

Then our "perp" almost gets caught by our team in the park. We've rattled his cage now, and I am afraid that he'll be back very soon to punish us when he finds out that his last intended victim is still with us! The most positive thing that comes out of all of this, is that he makes mistakes when he's under pressure.'

THIRTY.

Monday 8:00 am, the team was already busy digging out files on car thefts, previous killer types, trade dealers for stolen items etc.

Armed with the data the detectives set to work. Tim and Mac took off on the tracks of Jeff Markham and Craig Warren to ask for their DNA, this would be crucial now that they had some blood to compare. They were also interested in what they got up to on a daily basis.

Meanwhile, checking out the MO of the killer against previous files old and new, Keith and Sophie decided to split it up. Sophie would check out the last five years, and Keith would check further back in time.

Keith also had something else up his sleeve, his sister Maisy was a Detective sergeant in the London Met, so he had contacted her to run through any files that she could access. So hopefully between the three of them they should come up with some comparisons.

Barney and Duncan were already on the road, they had information about a "fence" from Gloucester, who has a reputation of dealing with the type of goods that were taken from the victims.

Sat at their desks trolling through car thefts and CCTV tapes, were Sharon and Bernie, assisted by WPC Elaine Carter a very competent user of the computer, a skill which they lacked. Elaine had been assisting the team for several weeks now, and she was hopeful of joining the CID herself one day, if the opportunity came up.

Tim and Mac had managed to track down Jeff Markham, working at a house that was being refurbished. He had informed them of his workplace when they brought him into the station on Sunday morning.

He had been reluctant to give his DNA sample at first, but then ran it over in his mind. The police were not after him for drug running, but suspicion of a mugging and theft, so he knew he was in the clear. He allowed the sample to be taken.

Craig Warren however gave them the slip when they arrived at the house. Contact with his employers only informed them that he was somewhere on the road, so say "cold calling" customers.

Tim and Mac decided to try later, and maybe catch him at home that evening.

By lunchtime Barney and Duncan were back at the incident room checking out details of another lead, their earlier one led nowhere. "The fence" (someone who deals in the buying and selling on of stolen goods), whose name was Johnny Pedersen alias "The Peddler" to his associates, was found to have nothing in connection to items of the victims and swore he had no knowledge of the stuff.

The car theft checks didn't turn up any reported thefts of a Vauxhall car linking to the earliest attack date, or since that time, but the CCTV tapes were showing a dark blue car in the areas close to where the attacks took place, but none were good enough to get a number plate shot yet, so they continued hopeful of a good shot with the visual checking of the tapes. This was a time consuming job, and tiring on the eyes.

The day passed without any ground being made, it was just a question of time, trolling through the information available and hoping something came out in the end.

Tuesday morning, Craig's fiancée Sarah and Kev's wife Lynn were at work having a mid morning coffee break together. Sarah was telling Lynn about Craig's moods, which of late were becoming more worrying to her; she couldn't get to the bottom of it. Whenever she broached the subject of his mood or temper, he would "go off on one".

'Perhaps his dad's illness is causing more stress than I realized!' said Sarah.

'When did you last speak with him about it?' asked Lynn.

'Not for a while now. Anyway, when I do ask he always changes the subject. He seems like he's in a world of his own sometimes and won't allow anyone in. I really think we're close to breaking up. We have been seeing less and less of each other over the last few months, but each time I ask him if there's a problem with our relationship, he says we're fine, and its just that his work and social life don't mix very well. I have even thought that he has someone else on the go!'

'Your not serious are you?' asked Lynn, shocked by her friend's comment.

'Well why not?' said Sarah. 'Take this last week. He says he has late night appointments so I don't get to see him for several nights. I look forward to going out at the weekend and getting together with him and our mates and look what happens? He throws a wobbler and storms out . . .

Do you know? He hasn't contacted me since that scene on Saturday night. I've called him and left messages on his mobile, but he hasn't answered me yet!'

'Have you been round his parents' house, he might be ill or something, you never know!' said Lynn.

'Too ill to answer his phone, or text messages? The truth is, I'm afraid to go round in case I find out he is seeing someone else, why can't he just tell me?'

Sarah was crying now and drawing attention to herself and Lynn as they sat in the coffee bar.

'I'll tell you what' said Lynn, 'I'll go with you tonight straight after work, and we'll get to the bottom of it, whether its to do with Craig's dad's illness, the stress of work, or another girl, we'll sort it tonight! Okay?'

'Okay . . .'

Tuesday lunchtime over a pint at "The Empty Jug", Craig was also the subject of the conversation between Spike, Dave and Danny.

'I don't know what's got into that boy!' said Danny. 'He has a lovely girl, a decent job and good mates, what more does he want?'

'He wants what we all want!' said Spike, being serious for a change.

'What's that then?' asked Dave.

'More!' said Spike, 'We all want more. More money, a better job, a bigger house, a faster car and in some cases a more beautiful woman. So the answer is more, right?'

'Well fuck me!' said Dave, 'I didn't ever have you down as a philosopher! But you could be right, I for one could certainly do with a bit more cash, and whilst I'm on the subject, we have another delivery tomorrow Dan. Our man is back a day early this week; I don't know why but got his text this morning. It said "10pm Wed @ udp." . . . , meaning 10:00 pm Wednesday at the usual drop point.

That means I probably won't have time to get back here with the gear, so I'll bring it over on Thursday, okay Dan?'

'Yeah, no problem' said Dan, 'just make sure Maggie doesn't see that we are still doing business okay.'

THIRTY ONE.

6:00 pm that evening at Craig's parents' house, Sarah and Lynn were welcomed in by Sylvia Warren, she was mid way through helping to feed Craig's father Arthur his early evening meal. Eating at the earlier hour helped with his digestion problems and allowed him to be more comfortable through the night.

'What brings you here at this time of the day darlin? Not that I'm unhappy to see you mind, but Craig's not home yet, in fact he won't be home for a week, I think he said.

I can't remember myself now.

I must be catching this Alzheimer thing off of this silly old bugger!' she said, throwing her thumb in the direction of her husband Arthur, who was sat with a napkin across his chest and staring into space, totally unaware of any visitors.

'A week!' said a stunned Sarah, 'but he . . .'

'Didn't he tell you luv? He said that he had to go on a training course or something, I don't know. But yeah, it was for the week I remember him telling me now.

Surely he told you, you must have forgotten, getting as bad as me and old dad eh?'

'Yeah, I seem to remember him saying something about it now' said Sarah, not wanting to upset or involve her future in-laws in any shit she had to contend with. They had enough on their plate already.

She turned and leaned over the table to speak to the old man.

'And how are you doing Arthur?'

'I'm doing fine, and I don't need any help from you lesbians!' he replied pointing at her and then Lynn.

Lynn instantly turned bright red and threw a hand over her mouth to stifle a laugh.

'Arthur!' shouted Sylvia, 'that's no way to talk to Sarah and her friend, now stop being an arsehole and eat your dinner!'

'Arseholes don't eat, they shit!' he came back with.

'My god' said Sylvia, embarrassed by the old man's comments, 'you see what Craig and I have to put up with? I'm so sorry Sarah.'

'Oh don't worry about us' said Sarah, 'we know he's unwell so we won't upset him anymore, we'll get out of the way and let him eat in peace.'

'Sorry to have disturbed you!' said Lynn.

'Bugger him!' said Sylvia, 'stay and have a cup of tea before you go, he won't even know you in five minutes anyway!'

They sat and chatted with Sylvia for half an hour while they drank tea. Sarah found out a few home truths from their little chit chat. Sylvia, absent mindedly, let slip the secret about the late nights that Craig was out "looking after street girls".

Sarah was shocked for the second time that afternoon, she now believed he was seeing someone else and using this bullshit excuse for his mother's sake. *'The bastard!'* she thought.

As they walked away from the house, Lynn put her arm around Sarah who was now sobbing loudly, there was no way back it seemed. Craig had someone else and didn't have the bollocks to tell her straight up.

The truth was, the only other love in Craig Warrens' life besides Sarah, was his deceased twin sister Carol. He loved Sarah as much as any man could love a woman, but he loved his sister more in that different kind of way that no one else would ever understand.

If only he could tell Sarah about Carol, but that could only lead to disaster. Sarah was inquisitive and would keep on at him until he told her everything, and he felt he was unable to do just that, so he had to distance himself from her somehow.

Now he sat in the dingy flat above the launderette, suddenly feeling very alone. He had to decide his next move.

Monday morning, the police had been asking questions at his workplace, and when Craig had rung his office to check on appointments, his boss asked him what the fuck was going on and told him to come in, he wanted a word!

Craig instantly knew his job would be over, his boss always made it clear that he would not accept any involvement with police matters.

Craig had phoned from Birmingham where he was having a meeting with "Freddy the fence", who was taking the latest items for cash. He had already managed to lose the unmarked police car at the house and a squad car on the way up country, which had tried to follow him, as they thought, to work.

After his meeting with Freddy, he had immediately gone to a Halfords outlet store and bought an all over car cover, he then drove back to the flat via "B roads" to avoid police on the motorway. He parked up around the back, concealed the car with the weatherproof cover tied down in place. He then went to the corner shop and bought enough food and milk to last a couple of days, then to the off license to buy some vodka.

He needed time to think, and the vodka would help.

The police were now convinced that Craig Warren definitely had something to hide.

Monday morning, after visiting his place of work, at least the place he worked out of, they found out that he should have gone in to work but didn't.

The usual procedure was that Craig went in to the offices on a Monday morning to sort out the weeks' appointments, and he then went on the road "cold calling" customers, to drum up extra clients.

This week he had not reported in, but called in mid morning by phone.

Earlier that morning detectives Clark and Mclean had gone to Warren's home to ask for the DNA sample, but as they arrived, Warren was pulling out of the drive in his car and had no intention of stopping; he knew they were police so he drove off at a fast pace. He was gone before they had chance to turn the car around and follow him.

Rather than give chase, they called control, gave them the registration and asked for all squad cars to be on the look out for his car.

A motorway team had followed him northbound for several miles and were awaiting instructions what to do, when an emergency call came in for an accident on the opposite carriageway, so priority dictated that they were pulled away to deal with that first.

Warren had slipped the net once more, and when the word got back to the station that Warren had given them the slip again, Dicky Williams was furious.

'Fucking uniform!' he said aloud 'couldn't catch a pig in a pen, the useless fuckers!'

There was a brief pause before he barked out some orders.

'Right, I want a search warrant for his parent's home ASAP. I want an unmarked car giving 24hr cover on that address, and tell them to park where it's not so fucking obvious! And I want people out there searching bars and anywhere he frequented; find out where he hangs out.

Come on you guys, lets step it up a bit!

How's that CCTV search coming along . . . Sharon? Bernie?'

'We're on it guv, but it's taking time to scan it properly, we don't want to miss anything so I'm afraid it can't be rushed. We have spotted the blue car within the crime scene areas as you know, but we are still trying for the license plate, then we can trace the bastard. I'm sure he won't be driving around unlicensed or uninsured. We're getting there guv!' said Bernie.

'Okay, let me know the minute you have that plate!'

'Alan!' he said to DS Hayes 'a word in my office please.'

The DCI regularly spoke alone with DS Hayes, he liked to bounce ideas off him, get a second opinion on things. He was a solid guy who would probably make chief inspector one day; Dicky had great respect for him as a colleague and a friend.

'The chief gets back tomorrow, he is going to expect a major breakthrough on this case, so I hope we can find that clue we are looking for before he gets here in the morning!'

'I'm sure we'll have something by then guv, the guys are doing everything possible, I think it's only a matter of time . . . Craig Warren looks favorite, the way he has been evading us and giving us the run around, and now it appears he has gone to ground somewhere.

Dave Douglas and Jeff Markham are out of the frame for the murders, but both are still under investigation. They both appeared to have something to hide, so I've asked uniform to have a dig around for us to see what they are up to.

A couple of guys volunteered to go plain clothes for a while so they could keep an eye on them.'

'That sounds good Al' said Dicky, 'The other thing I wanted to run by you, was that I'm thinking about passing over the story on Peter Sherman's attack to the press, and letting the attacker know that we now have a description of him. At least by doing that now, the chief might just understand the reason for withholding the story as it happened. What do you think?'

'I think that would be a wise move' said Alan. 'We have gained a little extra time from it now, and I don't see any advantage of stretching it out any further. Plus I'm sure the chief won't want anything untoward hanging around, that could compromise a verdict when we catch the fucker!

So, if we can wrap that up in a little package and pass it over to the press, all the better I say.'

'Right, I was hoping you would agree with my opinion, I'll sort out the press release right away, and we should see it in all the national morning papers. Hopefully the chief won't be in too early, and we may have a bit more news on "our boy" by then!'

THIRTY TWO.

Wednesday morning, the chief was in bright and early, much against DCI Williams' wishes; he could have done with more time to prepare for the onslaught of the tongue lashing he expected to receive.

The national newspapers had covered the story although it didn't make the front page. Dicky was however, surprised by the chief's composure and calm reserve as he brought him up to date with the latest information on current cases. He must have been on a stress control training week thought Dicky, because he would normally have blown his top already by the news he was listening to.

The Chief Constable listened intently and without interrupting his DCI, and gave him praise for the team's effort.

It was obvious to him that they were closing the net on the killer, and that it would be only a matter of time before they got their deserved result.

'Okay, thank you Derek' he said, 'You'll keep me informed won't you?' It was more of a statement than a request.

As DCI Williams walked back into the incident room after briefing the chief, everyone in the room suddenly dropped their heads and appeared to look extremely busy at their desks!

'Okay guys, you can relax' he said, 'I've managed to impress the chief, so now you have to impress me by giving me some results. I want an update every hour from now on. The pressure is on, and we're going to flush this fucker out of the woodwork, let's go to it!'

It was lunchtime, and WPC Elaine Carter was still trawling through the CCTV tapes whilst munching on a cheese and lettuce sandwich when, bingo!

She put her lunch to one side as she zoomed in on a piece of still footage showing the blue Vauxhall Vectra stopped at a traffic light junction.

Voila! there was the license plate number as plain as day on the screen. She gulped down the left over food in her mouth and swilled it down with coke.

She called Sharon and Bernie over to her desk excitedly; they too were eating, but came across to her to see what the commotion was about.

'I've got him!' she said ecstatically, pointing at the screen as she zoomed in to see the enlarged number plate.

'Look!'

As they came around to her side of the desk to see, DCI Williams was also on his way, he had heard the WPC's shout of glee from his office.

'She's found it guv, she's fucking found it!' said Sharon unable to contain her emotion.

'That's great work Elaine' said the DCI as he moved round to see the screen.

'Well done. Now let's see who it's registered to!'

She quickly had the registrations database on screen, typed in the registration number to let the data run through.

By now, everyone in the room had stopped what they were doing, and had somehow managed to encircle the WPC's desk. There were a few "whoops and yeah's" as the screen came up with the name and address.

The dark blue Vauxhall Vectra, private registration plate S872 DAD, belonged to Mr. Arthur James Warren. 56, Westleigh Gardens, Leckhampton, Cheltenham. Gloucestershire.

'That's Craig Warren's father!' exclaimed Sharon. 'But he has Alzheimer's!'

'Yeah, but Craig Warren doesn't, does he!' said Bernie.

'This is what we have been working for guys!' said Dicky.

'Okay . . . Sharon, Bernie Alan and myself will go round there.

Tim call the surveillance car over there, and tell them Craig Warren is our man, if he returns to the house to wait until we are there for back up, we don't want to frighten him off.

Mac, can you inform SOCO that we will need a team across there but to hold off around the corner from the house until we call them in . . . do we have that court order for the search of the premises yet?'

'Not yet guv' said Duncan, 'about another half an hour.'

'Make that ten minutes ago, we need it right now, so go get it!'

Twenty minutes later two squad cars pulled up in front of the Warren household. Craig Warren had not yet shown up.

The detectives moved in, Dicky and Alan to the front door, Sharon and Bernie to the rear in case Craig was at home and decided to make a break.

Only Sylvia and Arthur Warren were at home, Dicky handed the search warrant to Sylvia to read and informed her of the reason, but she was in shock at the thought of the police hunting down her son on suspicion of murder.

The detectives quickly did a room by room search in case Craig was hiding out somewhere, but he was not to be found in the house.

The back of the house had a high fence all the way around so was quite secure, it would take some effort to scale the fences, so they were happy there was no escape route to the back of the building.

Sharon and Bernie attained the keys to the locked outbuildings and garage. After checking that all the outbuildings were clear, there was just the garage to check, and they found what they had been after for so long, the Vauxhall Vectra car, possibly used by Craig when he ventured out on a killing spree.

They called in the SOCO team from round the corner; who quickly got to work on the car as well as Craig Warren's bedroom.

Dicky and Alan were in the sitting room with Sylvia Warren, she was frantically trying to tell them how good her son was, helping the lost girls on the streets.

Dicky was lending a sympathetic ear, but her efforts were futile, the evidence was now stacked well and truly against Craig Warren.

All they had to do now was to bring him in, and that was why Dicky was being patient with Sylvia.

The search of the house didn't turn up any of the stolen items or the clothing that Craig wore on his nights of revenge, so he must have another place somewhere and it was possible she knew where that was.

A little while later, a transporter arrived to take the car away to the police forensic compound, where it would undergo further investigation under controlled conditions. SOCO had almost immediately found synthetic strands of red and blonde hair from the wigs on the driver's seat.

Evidence bags were full of Craig Warren's personal items from his room; they too would be screened by forensics for trace evidence to compound the evidence against him.

Finally the detectives left the house, satisfied that there was nothing more that Mrs. Warren could tell them. A squad car and two uniformed officers was to remain posted near the house, but out of view. In fact they had been given permission by a nosey neighbour almost opposite the house, to use their driveway, and if they wanted, to use an upper floor room from which they would have a perfect sighting of the Warren house. They accepted gladly, a perfect stakeout in comfort for the officers.

It was near to 6:00 pm in the evening, and there had been no sighting of Craig Warren yet, the detectives could only assume he was holed up in his alternative accommodation.

Sarah, the fiancée had been brought in for questioning, and was as shocked as the mother had been when informed by DCI Williams of Craig's dark secret.

'No fucking way!' she screamed. 'It's not possible, I would have known, wouldn't I?'

But after being given a few brief details and dates of the attacks, it started to hit home to her that it could be true. She mentioned the helping of the street girls thinking that what Sylvia had told her could have been true. Oh how happy she would be if it were just that. She prayed it was true, and that this could all be a big misunderstanding, and that they had mistaken Craig for someone else.

She sat for a while, shell shocked, and her world blown to pieces. The man she loved and trusted is possibly a cold blooded serial killer. It sent a shiver down her spine.

She of course, had no idea of his current whereabouts or his secret hideaway either.

'We'll also need to talk to your friends from "The Empty Jug", it's possible that someone close may know where he is . . . who is Craig's closest mate Sarah?'

'Uum . . . well they're all good close friends, so I don't really know who Craig would confide in, I'm sorry!' she burst into tears at that point.

The DCI said she should go home and that he would call her when they find him.

After she had left, he sent Barney and Duncan to 'The Empty Jug' to round up the guys who know Craig.

Later that evening, Keith received a call from his sister Maisy who had been trolling through archived files at the London Met; she had found something, and was about to fax the details across to him.

He sat drinking coffee as he waited by the fax machine.

After about ten minutes it kicked into motion, and spewed out the sheets of information.

He picked up the first sheet and began reading it, while the rest of the pages continued to print and slide out of the fax-printer machine and into the receiving tray.

The first few paragraphs held some crucial information.

'Oh fuck!' He said aloud.

THIRTY THREE.

Dave Douglas finished work Wednesday evening at five thirty, but by the time he got home after being held up by the rush hour traffic, it was closer to six.

Karen had arrived home only minutes before him, and had started preparing the evening meal of corned beef hash with peas, carrots and a thick gravy which was Dave's favorite.

Dave made them both a cup of tea, and then sat at the breakfast bar drinking and chatting to Karen. She knew he had a delivery coming in tonight and wished that he would give it up; they could manage with what they already earned, and could just cut back on a few nights out and eat a little cheaper.

Dave wouldn't hear of it though, he said that he was just a little fish and that the authorities were more interested in the bigger players, all he was doing was selling a few thousand ciggy's without paying the tax which, he said, was peanuts compared to what some people get away with.

Besides no one other than Danny knew when the stuff came over, and even he didn't know where the pickups took place, only Dave and the driver knew that. It was safe. The drop off tonight was a day earlier than usual, but it didn't make any difference to Dave what night it came in.

They sat together and ate their meal when it was ready, then Dave had a snooze in his comfy leather chair in front of the TV before it was time to go to the pick up point.

Four uniformed officers from the Cheltenham station, had volunteered for the plain clothes duty, two were assigned to keeping an eye on Dave Douglas and the other two were reporting back on Jeff Markham.

PC's Grant Statham and Simon Howell had been watching Douglas, and after following him home they returned to the station where they had received information from a Customs and Excise contact, who himself had been informed by a colleague on the Calais side.

It was regarding a lorry coming from France which was carrying an excessive amount of cigarettes that were concealed amongst some industrial farm machinery parts. The lorry was allowed to pass through customs on the French side so that actions could be put in place before it arrived on the English side. The paperwork informed them that the lorry was destined to deliver the parts to none other than Dave Douglas's employers' warehouse.

They had a description of the lorry and what the goods were, but no idea if the contraband would be dropped off before the warehouse delivery.

Statham and Howell had reported this back to DS Hayes who, although busy enough with the Warren case, decided he needed to be part of the team to swoop on Douglas this very evening.

So having cleared it with DCI Williams to go ahead, he was also advised to involve Customs and Excise to assist with the operation, as it was very likely that it was going to be their baby anyway.

If it was in any way to do with importing illegal goods or import tax evasion. 'Let them have the glory and the paperwork on that one!' said Dicky.

DS Hayes and several uniformed officers formulated a plan along with the C&E, to work together in catching the offenders. Two officers from the Dover constabulary along with two C&E officers would follow the lorry from the port once it arrived, while the DS and three other officers from Cheltenham would locate Douglas and follow him.

It was agreed that the police would do the initial swoop on the lorry as the handover was in progress, and then the Customs guys would attend and check out the shipment and the required paperwork.

If there was any non compliance with importing etc, then the C&E would take it over and continue the processing of the shipment and the people involved.

At the moment it appeared that there was only Dave Douglas and the foreign driver involved. It was hoped that there would not be more people at the drop, otherwise they may have a job containing the offenders at the scene.

The DS was happy that the eight officers should be able to contain the situation between them.

The team following the lorry would drive on past if the lorry pulled in anywhere, then having turned around would drive back past the lorry and pull in off the road to observe any movements. If Douglas drove to the warehouse there was a chance that the cigarettes would be dropped off there as well. If not, then he may meet at a drop off point at another location with the lorry.

They planned radio contact between the teams at all times during the task. The plan was to have officers ready to storm the warehouse should the drop be there, or block in the lorry and Douglas's car if it was another location, then move in.

'It should be a straight forward operation,' quoted a young Custom's and Excise officer to Detective Sergeant Hayes.

'I bloody well hope so!' said the DS. 'I've had too many late nights the last few months, and I could do with a quick in and out operation!'

The teams were both in place by 7:30 pm, and a radio message from the port team said the lorry was on the way. It would be around two and a half hours before it reached the warehouse, so it would be a long wait watching Douglas's house until he made a move.

Waiting time on these sort of stakeouts always dragged by, so Alan Hayes always took coffee and sandwiches to see him through, but tonight was a bit of a rush and he had none, so he did a radio check with the other car every fifteen minutes, it helped to pass the time.

At 9:20 pm, Dave Douglas came out of his house and got into his blue Ford estate car and drove off in the direction of the warehouse.

The unmarked squad car followed, and the DS informed the other team, who in turn confirmed that they were approximately forty five minutes away if the drop off was at the warehouse.

Ten minutes later the DS informed the other team that Douglas was not going to the warehouse, so the drop must be somewhere on the incoming route of the lorry.

Both teams continued to tail their respective vehicles.

Half an hour from the warehouse, the lorry pulled into a lay-by and the following team drove on past.

Further up the road they turned the car around and drove back past the stationary vehicle, they then parked off the road to observe the lorry driver. The team leader informed the DS that the white 35ton box wagon was static in a lay-by and gave their approximate position.

The DS calculated that they were only minutes away, so they eased back some way so that they would be able to pull in before the lay-by.

About three minutes later, Dave Douglas pulled into the lay-by and backed his estate car up to the rear of the lorry to make the unloading easier.

The tail gate of the lorry was opened up as the car backed up to it. Douglas got out and greeted the lorry driver before he opened the tail door of the estate car.

The C&E car had a good view of what was going on, they informed DS Hayes that the unloading had begun and that it was almost certainly boxes of cigarettes.

The DS gave the word and the squad cars moved in from each side, screeching to a halt boxing in the two vehicles, the officers were out of the cars shouting instructions at the two men unloading the lorry.

Dave and the lorry driver were taken totally by surprise and were rooted to the spot. The officers moved in on them, reading them their rights and then putting on the restraints.

The driver was asked for the cargo invoices, he told an officer where to find them in the cab, the problem was, there was paperwork for the engineering equipment he had on board, but not for the sixty thousand cigarettes that they were unloading into the back of Dave Douglas's car.

They both knew they were in deep shit!

After being taken to the station, they were both charged and later released to await a court hearing. There was a possibility that they would face a custodial sentence, even though it was a first offence for them both, but that would be down to the prosecution services to decide.

Dave Douglas was pulled aside after being charged and released; he was led into an interview room for questioning about his friend Craig Warren.

His head was in a spin, first getting caught red handed with the cargo of cigarettes, and now what?

DS Hayes wanted to ask him a few questions about Craig Warren before he was let go.

'Mr Douglas, You've provided an exciting evenings entertainment so far, so how about I give you a chance to redeem yourself?' said Hayes.

'Anything . . . I'll do anything if I can keep my job!' spluttered Douglas.

'I didn't say anything about keeping your job sir, I just want some honest answers to a few questions.'

'But it might help me right?' Douglas said with hope.

'Let's get down to the questions first . . . now, do you have a best mate called Craig Warren?'

'Uh . . . yeah, but I swear he has nothing to do with the ciggy's, he's just a good mate that's all!'

'This has nothing to do with the cigarettes . . . do you know if Craig has another residence somewhere, other than his parents' house?'

'Another place? I don't know what you mean?' said Douglas, totally confused by the question.

'It's quite a simple question Mr Douglas, does Craig Warren have a second home, somewhere other than his parents' house where he normally resides . . . Perhaps an apartment or a bedsit?'

'No . . . I mean, not that I know of, he can barely afford to get by living at home let alone the expense of somewhere else. No, I would say definitely not.'

'Okay,' said Hayes, 'what about your other mates from the pub, is there someone who is closer to Craig, more of a confidant than you might be?'

'Uh . . . no I don't think so, we all get on about the same I think . . . what's this all about anyway? Is he in trouble or something?'

'Oh yes, he's definitely in trouble Mr Douglas.'

DS Hayes told him that Warren was wanted in connection with the knife attacks in the city.

Dave Douglas was totally shocked at the news; this surely wasn't the Craig he knew!

'Craig? . . . you're joking . . . no never, it can't be him, I'll stake my life on it!' said Douglas.

'I'm afraid we have overwhelming evidence Mr Douglas, your friend is wanted for multiple murders.'

Shortly after the shocking news Dave Douglas was released, DS Hayes was satisfied he knew nothing judging by his reaction to the news.

The cargo of cigarettes was confiscated by the Customs & Excise officers, and they would be dealing with the case from here, with help from the crown prosecution.

Dave Douglas and the driver both knew that it would be the end of their employment with the company. It's not really a good example having employees charged with import tax evasion when you're an importing company!

During the questioning, Dave never mentioned that anyone else was involved, he made sure that he kept Danny out of trouble, and there was no point in escalating the blame. At least he can say that he protected his mates.

DS Hayes had thanked everyone for doing a good job; thankfully this was one job that went as planned.

The guys from Dover were happy with the assistance from the Gloucestershire squad, and they would take it from here.

Once away from the station, Douglas phoned Danny and informed him of the takedown.

Although shocked and sorry for Dave, Danny was also slightly relieved that it was over. He immediately disposed of any packets of ciggy's with the foreign warning printed on them, which he had left over.

He didn't want the police to find any trace of them at the pub.

THIRTY FOUR.

Thursday morning, Alan Hayes gave a verbal report to Dicky about the success of the previous night's combined operation with the Customs & Excise guys, it had all gone to plan and Dicky praised his DS.

There was still no sign of Craig Warren. The evidence that Keith's sister Maisy had sent by fax from the London Met file archives, would without doubt be the final nail in the coffin for Craig Warren.

The file contained information about the murder of Carol Warren, one of seven women, all prostitutes, who were attacked and killed by a crazed knife wielding doctor.

Carol was the seventh victim on the list of names.

DS Hayes, DC Keith Butler and DC Sophie Smith were listening while DCI Williams read the documented details out loud.

The file read:-

'The 36 year old Doctor, Adam Gillespie GP and his wife Irene 34, were married for nearly six years, then they separated after Irene was unable to conceive.

His obsession with having a son had driven her away.

A statement from Doctor Gillespie, claimed that after the split he turned to having sexual relationships with prostitutes.

Then six months after parting from his wife, he was struck off the medical register for professional misconduct, after the attempted rape of a patient.

He was sentenced to 18months in prison. The loss of his wife had also had a serious effect on his mental health, and he eventually had a nervous breakdown while still in custody.

After completing his jail sentence, he returned to the streets and suffered another breakdown.

While undergoing treatment for his second mental breakdown, he killed his first victim, who was one of the street girls he regularly had sex with. She had her abdomen cut open and her carotid artery cut, as did the following six victims.

The doctor was finally caught, when an attempt on the life of another prostitute, which would have been his eighth victim, was foiled by a passer-by who managed to apprehend him until the police arrived.

In Gillespie's statement, he claimed he thought that one of the prostitute girlfriends was pregnant, and he told her that if it was a boy that she carried, then he would marry her. She had told him that he was crazy, and that she wasn't even pregnant . . .

He freaked out, and sliced her open to find out if she was lying to him, he cut her throat to stop her screams. He of course found that she was not carrying his baby.

He then went on to commit the same attacks on the other girls that he had been with, one by one he cut them open, trying to find the baby son he thought they were concealing from him!'

'That's one mad son of a bitch!' said Sophie.

'Was!' said the DCI, 'he was being subjected to tests by a psychiatrist to validate his plea of insanity, when he took his own life. Apparently he managed to secrete a sharp item on his person, and when he was allowed to use a bathroom he slit his own throat, he bled to death in minutes!'

'Jesus! Now we know why Craig Warren is killing these men' said DS Hayes, 'he's using the same MO as Gillespie, only he's killing men who go near prostitutes because his sister was one . . . and she was also a victim of this nutter!'

'Exactly!' said Dicky.

THIRTY FIVE.

PC Rory Walker and PC Gary Davis had been closely tracking Jeff Markham for two days now to no avail, but they know that this evening he may show his hand if he is up to something, because they suspect that he possibly has dodgy dealings and connections at "Cleo's club", they will be following him there tonight!

At the moment they're sitting in an unmarked police car taking it in turns to tell jokes to pass the time. Then in turn they go for a walk to stretch the legs and peer into the building where Markham was still at work plastering walls, making sure he hasn't spotted them and done a runner out of the back door.

At lunchtime he ventured no further than the "Westchester Arms" for a pie and a pint, then back to work after an hour or so.

Meanwhile in his hideaway flat, Craig Warren was going stir crazy and decided he had to get out of this place, maybe move up country somewhere and start all over.

First though, he thought he owed it to his parents to let them know he was okay.

He would go home, pack some personal things and write a letter for Sarah. Say goodbye to his mum and dad, and then disappear up north, perhaps Yorkshire or somewhere rural for a while.

First of all, he was going to take all the clothes he had used for his disguises and burn them in the oil drum outside. He had no valuables left to pawn; there was nothing of value left in the flat. Last of all he would ditch the scalpel somewhere safe . . .

No; he decided against that, he might need it again.

He took the clothes down the backstairs to the oil drum, dropped them in and set fire to them, occasionally poking and turning the burning remains to make sure they were burnt beyond recognition. Afterwards he walked around to the corner shop where he bought some fresh cakes, milk and a newspaper, then returned to the flat.

While he made some coffee he flicked through the pages of the newspaper. On page four was a column on the knife attacks. He read it carefully, more than once, especially the part where it claimed that the police now had a witness who had come forward, and could identify the killer.

It also said that the story was a follow up to yesterday's story.

He quickly returned to the corner shop. 'Where are your newspapers from yesterday?' he said to the shopkeeper, who was looking a little confused at the question.

'What part of my question don't you understand?' he barked. 'Yesterdays newspapers, do you have any here that were left over? Unsold?'

'Oh . . . yeah, I have a few out back which didn't sell, which one do you want? I think there are some "Daily Mirror", some "Sun", oh and "The Cheltenham Echo" out there!' said the man.

'All of 'em, one of each!' said Warren pulling his hand out of his pocket with some money in it.

The man went out to the back of the shop, returning with the three different newspapers and gave them to Warren.

'You can have them, no charge.' he said.

Warren snatched them up and rushed out of the shop door, papers held under his arm.

'Oh thank you sir! . . . Anytime sir! . . . Ignorant fucker!' said the shopkeeper.

Back in the privacy of his flat, Warren quickly poured himself vodka and sat at the kitchen table reading through the stories on page two, all of which were almost identical, meaning they probably came from a blanket press release.

As he read about Peter Sherman's attack and the fact that he was still alive, his temper was boiling. 'So, those fuckers tricked me into thinking he was dead!' He said aloud to himself.

The story outlined the attack and injuries sustained by Sherman, yet he had given the police a full description of his attacker, it said that they had a suspect whom they had not yet apprehended. A computer generated likeness of the alleged attacker was alongside the story column. Warren thought that although not exact, it was a definite resemblance and people would recognize it as him.

He remembered on the night, that his makeup had run down his face, and he had the wig pulled off as they struggled after that kick in the bollocks!

The couple running towards him, then plunging of the knife to the man's gut, and yet he still survived?

'*Could the interfering bastards have been police?*' He thought. His mind was racing through the events, and the more he ran through it, the more he was convinced it was the police who chased him that night. The woman had run to help that prick on the floor, and the man had followed himself only as far as the outside of the gate to he park.

He remembered watching the man from his hiding place behind a driveway hedge, holding the blade ready; he was no more than twenty metres away, if he had followed on up the road he would have also been lying in his own offal. But the coward had turned and gone back to the bitch, she must have saved the tosser on the ground!

In his temper, Warren threw the empty vodka glass at the wall, smashing it into little pieces. Then as cool as anything, he got up and finished making the coffee.

He sat and devoured the fresh cakes and coffee, feeling like he needed to build his energy for what was to come.

Afterwards, he sat working out a new plan, he would have to contend with the police hunting him now and his idea of going north was going to be difficult.

He would have to change his car because they would know the registration by now, he would just leave it where it was, under the tarpaulin.

'*What about going home?*' he thought.

'A taxi!' he said aloud, 'I'll get a taxi, do a drive past the house to see if it's safe, then go in and out quickly before police have time to react . . .

Shit!

I could have dressed as Carol, they won't be expecting a girl to call at the house, and now I just burnt all the clothes . . . bollocks!'

'*Never mind, there's a way around that*' he thought.

Timing was going to be critical, and tonight under the cover of darkness would give him the edge. So as not to waste time at the house, he decided that he would write the letter for Sarah while he waited to go.

He walked round the corner to the charity shop in the next road and purchased an outfit along with shoes and a brown wig.

The old woman in the shop made some comment about how men didn't usually come in and buy second hand clothes for their wives, Craig made light of it by saying he was going to a fancy dress party as a lady of the night.

The old lady had laughed and said, 'you'll be the smartest lady boy there!'

On his way back to the flat, he went to his car and removed his briefcase and anything he needed before locking it up and throwing the cover back over it.

Yes it was best he left the car here, it would be some time before anyone would realize it was dumped, and by then he would be long gone.

He tossed the keys as far as he could, over the fence into the long grass beyond.

He pondered a moment longer then pulled out his mobile phone. There were five unread messages on it.

Without reading the messages he dismantled the phone, then he tossed the sim card and the pieces of phone over the fence as far as he could throw them, then he walked back to compose his letter to Sarah.

THIRTY SIX.

Jeff Markham came out of his house that evening around 7:30 pm, and walked round to "The Westchester Arms" where he met up with his buddies.

At 8:30 pm, they all came out of the pub and walked directly to "Cleo's club". The two PC's followed them in and tried to blend in with the crowd so they could watch Markham.

For an hour or so he did nothing much except talking and drinking with his mates, then he broke away and was in amongst a mixed group of men and women.

From where they were watching, the PC's could see something changing hands for money, and it wasn't long before they confirmed it was drugs.

Rory Walker had decided to approach Markham, saying that he wanted some of what he was selling; he told him that he had a friend who had recommended him for selling "good stuff".

It cost Rory twenty quid for a small packet, and judging on the amount of people going to Markham, he was making a mint here at the club. The bouncers were turning a blind eye, after Markham had slipped the two of them a packet each. The punters were buying the gear and heading straight for the toilets, and then blatantly returning to the main bar area with the residue still around their noses.

Rory and Gary decided to call it in and see how the guv'nor wanted them to play it.

The desk sergeant put them through to DS Hayes who listened to the report; he needed to speak to DCI Williams first, and said he would get back to them shortly.

After ten minutes he called them back, he instructed them to hold back and just observe Markham's movements for now, it was possible he may lead them back to the supplier which would be a greater result.

For some time Markham continued to hand out the small packets for cash, until finally he must have sold all he had, and he returned to be with his mates for a final drink before leaving the club.

It was only 10:55 pm as he was leaving the club; it looked like he was heading home. Walker and Davis followed and watched him enter his house, expecting him to come back out reloaded with bags and then possibly go back to the club.

He did come out eventually, but got into his car and drove off. He had caught them cold, but luckily they had managed to get his registration number, but now they had no chance to catch up with him because their own vehicle was parked up around the corner.

'Shit!' said Rory, 'DS Hayes is going to be pissed off, now that we've lost him!'

Gary just grimaced and shook his head.

Rory called in the news to DS Hayes, and then had to hold the phone away from his ear due to the high pitched abuse coming from it.

Hayes quickly had a bulletin put out from the station radio room to all cars, to be on the lookout for Markham's car.

Lucky for Walker and Davis, the car was spotted by an unmarked patrol car as it headed out of Cheltenham on the Gloucester road, and the patrol car was now following a short distance behind Markham.

The suspect's car had driven into an area of Down Hatherley, and pulled into a short off-road driveway and up to the gates of a large rural property, which had CCTV cameras set on top of the pillars supporting the gates to the wide entrance.

As the unmarked car drove past, the officers observed Markham, still seated in his car, talking into the security speaker mounted on the right hand pillar.

Seconds later, the gates opened automatically and Markham drove up the driveway to the front of the house, the gates then closed behind him.

The officers parked up the road from the property, but they had a slightly obscured view to the front door of the house from where they were sitting.

They called the station and spoke to Hayes, who had their position passed on to Walker and Davis; they would drive over there and relieve the unmarked car then continue their observation of Markham at the house.

Meanwhile, DS Hayes had someone check out the Down Hatherley address to find out who owned such a prestigious property.

A short while later, the DS was informed that it belonged to a Mr Robert Morgan, a wealthy businessman who owns a landscape gardening business, which is run from a garden centre that he also owns on the Tewkesbury road.

'The plot thickens!' he said, to the young policewoman who handed him the results of the identity search.

THIRTY SEVEN.

At the same time as Jeff Markham had left his home at around 7:30 pm, Craig Warren was preparing to go and see his parents, dressed up in his new disguise.

As he checked the look of his wig and makeup in the bathroom mirror, he wondered how much longer he could go on like this. Now that the police were after him, he knew he would never be able to walk around freely, or without looking over his shoulder to see if he was being followed. They would eventually put the pieces together and he would be locked away forever.

He straightened up and stood back, looking in the mirror with a crack in it, then he walked back into the lounge and stood in front of the photo of himself and Carol which was propped up on the chest of drawers.

'I can't give myself up!' he said, 'I have to go north and rebuild my life, without you and without Sarah. I just need to go, I'm sorry Carol!'

He called a taxi, and five minutes later was on his way to his parents' house.

The taxi driver kept giving him strange glances in his rearview mirror, which he half expected. There was no conversation between them, apart from directions to the house.

Once there, he told the driver he should turn around at the end of the road, come back along and pull up outside the house and wait for him.

The driver agreed, but said that the meter would be running the whole time.

Craig just said, 'Don't worry, I'll give you a big tip for doing as I ask, and no questions.'

The driver just nodded, smiled and thought to himself, '*I don't really care you queer fucker, its easy money for me!*'

As the taxi pulled around the corner into the road, Craig told the driver to slow down and turn around at the other end.

As they moved slowly up the road, Craig was paying particular attention to upper windows and driveways to see if he could spot the police. He didn't see anything unusual, however, he knew they would be close; he would have to be in and out of his parents' house quickly.

Chances were that the house was being staked out, and the officers would have to call for backup before making a move, so that should give him enough time. Also, he had his disguise, and that would fuck with their brains for a few more minutes.

He was right in his thinking of course, the house was under surveillance.

One of the two officers watching from the upstairs window of the nosey neighbour's house across the road, watched as the taxi drove past and went up the road, turned around and come back to stop outside the Warrens' house.

The officer who was taking his turn at the time to watch through binoculars and a zoom lens camera, which were set up behind white netted curtained windows, informed his stakeout partner of some action.

His partner was currently tucking into his second large piece of home made current cake, and slurping on a cup of the endless supply of tea. After putting down his snack, he moved across to the camera, while his buddy eyed the visitor using the bin's.

As the taxi parked up outside his parents' house, Craig pulled up the collar on his ladies raincoat that he was wearing, and stepped out of the car.

He moved quickly up the driveway to the front door and rang the doorbell to make it look like he was a visitor. Sylvia Warren came to open the door, and as soon as it was open Craig walked straight past her into the house, telling her to shut the door quickly.

The stakeout crew were discussing between themselves who they thought the woman who had just turned up in the taxi could be.

'Perhaps it's a relative come to give the old couple some support eh?' said the one officer to the other.

'Who the hell are you?' said Silvia Warren to the stranger who had just pushed her way inside . . .

Craig turned to face her. 'It's me mum . . . Craig!'

A look of shock appeared on her face. 'Jesus Christ . . . is that really you son?'

'Yes mum it is, but don't worry, it's for a good reason. But I don't have time to explain now, I just need to grab some clothes before I go okay!'

'Go where Craig, the police are after you?' she pleaded.

'I can't say. The less you know the better, that way the police will leave you alone!' he said, climbing the stairs two at a time.

He quickly shoved some clothes into a sports hold-all bag, along with some other keepsakes including another picture of Carol and himself.

As he turned to leave the bedroom, his mother stood in the doorway. 'Why son?' she said.

'Because I said I have to go away.' Craig said.

'No . . . why did you kill all those innocent men?'

There was silence, and Craig sat on the bed. Tears welled in his eyes as he looked at his old mum standing there, proud and strong as ever.

'For Carol' he said quietly, 'I did it all for Carol . . . I did it to all those bastards who use helpless girls and then treat them like shit on their shoes. They all fucking deserved it mum . . . they did!'

'No Craig they didn't, it's just a way of life that people choose. Killing those men won't bring Carol back, the scumbag who killed her is dead now but that makes no difference either, because we still feel the pain of loss.

Killing doesn't ever stop that.

So you have to stop now Craig, give yourself up, you need help, and you know I will always do what I can to help you. No matter what you've done, you're still my son!'

'I love you mum, but I can't give myself up. I couldn't live a life of being locked up in a cell, taking the abuse from the guards, or worse, a mental institution like the last time I was ill.

Being doped up with drugs all the time, and where the nursing staff beat, torture and even rape men and women alike. They committed worse crimes than the in-patients . . . no, I'm going away to start afresh, free and able to call or write to you anytime I want.

I promise I will keep in touch mum, but I must go now before it's too late!'

He rose from the bed, hugged his mother then kissed her on the forehead. He picked up his bag, and as he went down the stairs his mother said,

'Where will you go?'

Craig just said, 'I'll write to you mum, I promise.'

Sylvia Warren wiped her eyes with her handkerchief and said, 'be careful son, the police are in a house across the road watching, I've seen them at the upstairs window of Mrs Wilkins' house.'

Meanwhile, it had taken a while for the clues to register to the surveillance men, that if someone was visiting they wouldn't ask the taxi to wait, they would call another when ready to leave. So whoever it was, would be coming out shortly and could possibly be picking up stuff for Craig Warren.

After calling HQ, DCI Williams had twigged it straight away, that it could be Craig Warren himself, so he instructed the officers to move in if the person came back out to the taxi.

Back up was on the way!

Craig now looked up at his mother who was standing at the top of the stairs. 'Goodbye mum, and thanks for everything. I love you. Tell dad . . .'

His voice trailed off, he didn't know what else to say. He placed the letter for Sarah on the narrow hallway table.

As he walked down the drive from the house, the taxi driver was stood leaning back against the door of his car smoking a cigarette. As he saw Craig coming, he dropped it to the floor and mashed it with his toe.

'About fucking time too!' He said as he turned to open the driver's door to get in. Craig ignored the taxi driver's remarks, but heard the shouts from the police officers who were approaching from the driveway of the house opposite.

'Police . . . Stay where you are!'

The taxi driver looked up from the car to see two men coming across the road towards him.

'What the fu . . . ?' He didn't get the words out before he felt the searing pain in his lower back where the knife went in.

Craig had pre-empted the police officers' move, and had unsheathed the scalpel ready in his hand as he approached the car. His only option now was to steal the taxi and get away.

He dropped his bag and pulled the falling driver to one side, allowing himself room to get in the car and lock the doors.

The officers were now banging on the windows shouting for him to get out of the car, but Craig started the engine and roared off up the road and out of sight.

The taxi driver was on the pavement, already in a pool of blood, bleeding heavily from his wound.

One of the officers called for an ambulance, while the other attended to the man.

Craig Warren had once again given the police a run for their money, but had left his bag behind in doing so. No problem, he could soon get some other clothes, it didn't matter, all he had to do now was put some distance between himself and the Cheltenham area.

He drove the car out towards Gloucester, then got on the M5 at the Golden Valley junction, and headed north.

He knew he would have to ditch the car and get a change of clothes, because pretty soon he would have the whole of the Gloucestershire police force out looking for him, and the taxi was a bit of a give away.

Maybe a services station on the motorway would provide for both his needs.

THIRTY EIGHT.

DCI Williams and DS Hayes were at the Warren's house, the scene of the attack on the taxi driver. The stabbed man was being transported to hospital with a puncture wound to his kidney.

Meanwhile, the two detectives were sat with Silvia Warren in the lounge.

WPC Elaine Carter was given the task of entertaining Arthur Warren, and he was in a playful mood for a change.

'What did your son come back here for Mrs Warren?' the DCI asked Silvia Warren.

'For his tea, and for some clothes, he has to go on another of those training courses, you know, for his job, so he'll be away for a while.' she replied casually.

DS Hayes moved directly in front of Sylvia and stooped down to look her in the eyes, he took both of her hands in his and said gently.

'Come on Mrs Warren, you don't have to play the innocent with us now, because we know very well that you're covering for him . . . now, please tell us where he's going, or do you want another death on your conscience? . . . you know he needs help, and we need to protect the public from him . . . help us to stop this insane revenge killing . . . please!'

She looked into the eyes of the Detective, she knew he was right. She reached into the pocket of her apron for her handkerchief, to dry her eyes for the second time that day, but there was nothing she could give them; Craig wouldn't say where he was going, only that he was going away.

She really didn't have any idea where, but she did tell them of the letter that Craig had left on the table. An officer was told to bag it and take it to the station.

Back at the incident room, the detectives were waiting for news on the whereabouts of the taxi cab, it had not been spotted since leaving the scene at the Warrens' house, but it would only be a matter of time.

The county police were on full alert for the vehicle with the armed and dangerous Craig Warren onboard. Once seen, the orders were to follow but not to attempt apprehending until full backup was on hand.

The time was 11:15 pm when DS Hayes had taken the call from PC Walker regarding Jeff Markham giving them the slip.

He had gone ballistic on the phone, mainly because they had managed to lose two suspects from separate cases tonight.

He had then instructed the radio communications officer to put out another vehicle registration that was needed in connection of a crime, again to follow not apprehend.

Ten minutes later, an unmarked car had spotted the car driven by Jeff Markham and had tailed it towards Down Hatherley. The patrol officers called in when the car was stationary at the address in Down Hatherley, which Det. Hayes then asked a junior WPC to check out.

After speaking with DCI Williams, DS Hayes contacted Walker and Davis and gave them instructions to observe and take notes only, who, what, why and when, a person or persons came into contact with Markham.

His last instruction to the PC's was, 'lose them again and you will never father any children, I will have your balls in a glass cabinet for all to see! Comprend`e?'

Rory Walker swallowed hard before answering.

'Yes sir, we do.'

Putting the phone down Hayes turned to Dicky, 'Those fucking plods get worse you know!'

DCI Williams pulled out two glasses and a bottle from a drawer in his desk. He poured a finger of scotch into each glass, then sat down.

'It's been a long day Al, and we got bigger fish to fry tonight!'

Alan raised his glass.

'Your right' he said, then gulped down the single malt.

Before the taste of scotch had dispersed in their mouths DC Barney Miller had knocked and entered the inspector's office.

'Guv, motorway police have found the stolen taxi at the Droitwich service station on the M5 northbound.'

'What about Warren?' the DCI asked anxiously.

'No sign guv . . . but we do have another body!'

Both detectives drained to a whiter shade of pale. 'Fuck it!' said Dicky. 'Who is it?'

'No I.D. yet guv, in fact the guy was found with no clothes or anything. The motorway boys found him behind one of the outer buildings while they were looking for Warren. It looks like Warren killed him, then he stole his clothes and I.D. and probably his car. The tarts clothes Warren had been wearing were left on the ground near the dead guy!'

'We better get up there quick Al, arrange a couple of cars and people while I call Worcester HQ and talk to my old mate Bert Saunders up there. We also need to find out the identity of the dead guy ASAP, so that we can trace the car.'

At the motorway services, the crime scene was cordoned off. SOCO were already there, along with the county coroner.

DCI Williams expected to encounter another bloody scene, not unlike the others that Warren had dispatched.

He was surprised at what he saw before him, not a spec of blood was to be seen anywhere. The coroner was quick to identify that the man had quite probably died of strangulation due to the markings around the throat.

'Well that makes sense,' said Dicky to Alan, 'he wouldn't want his new clothes covered in blood would he? And no witnesses either I suppose? Warren is a clever fucker, I'll give him that!'

The detectives left the crime scene for SOCO to do their stuff. The best chance they had to see the train of the events would be the CCTV.

An officer from Worcester had already picked up the tapes from all CCTV cameras covering the last three hours.

At Worcester police HQ, the detectives worked together with the locals to trawl through the tapes and find their man.

Once they found the taxi on the tapes it was easy. The car park cameras covered the whole area and they were able to track Warren's movements.

He had sat in the taxi for nearly half an hour waiting for the right guy to come along, and then he could be seen following a man towards the outbuilding, where the body was later found.

He had probably attacked the man from behind with a scarf, wrapping it around his neck and dragging him around the back of the building, then re-emerging several minutes later dressed in the dead man's clothes.

By tracking the victim back to his car, prior to the attack, the detectives were able to see the registration and access the man's identity. They also tracked Warren to the same car after he strangled the driver.

The registration of the car was quickly broadcast across the counties, to all motorway, urban and rural patrol cars.

Warren would not be aware how quickly the police had moved to retrieve this vital information, so there was a good chance he would not try to change his car again just yet.

Hopefully not before they tracked him down anyway.

SOCO did a quick check of the stolen Taxi, and found a blood soaked scalpel in the driver's side foot-well of the car. Warren must have dropped it on the floor of the Taxi when he got in, after stabbing the driver.

THIRTY NINE.

Walker and Davis were still keeping watch on the house they were told was owned by a Robert Morgan. There had been no movement at the house since they arrived about two hours ago, but three men had just come outside, causing the security lights to come on which illuminated the whole front of the property and driveway. They had walked around to the side of the house.

Gary pulled out the camera with the telephoto lens fitted. A few minutes later, he zoomed in on the three men as they reappeared from the side of the house, one of them was Markham, and one of the other two they assumed to be Morgan, the third was unknown. Gary took facial shots of each one.

He also took shots of Markham carrying a sports bag and putting it into the boot of his car, then after shaking hands with the other two men, he and the unknown man got into their own cars and drove towards the gate one behind the other.

The man they believed to be Robert Morgan appeared to open the gate with a remote control, and once the cars had driven out, closed the gates and returned inside the house.

Gary had the shots of the people, the cars and registrations, all before Rory started the car ready to tail Markham, who drove past their parked car, heading back towards Cheltenham.

Back at his house, Markham removed the sports bag from the boot of his car and proceeded inside the house. His lights went on, and within an hour went off. They had to assume he had gone to bed, but waited a further thirty minutes before leaving.

They were both absolutely knackered; they had been out since early hours tailing the son of a bitch, now it was time to rest up until morning.

Friday morning in the CID incident room, everyone was on alert. News from the hospital was that the taxi driver was stable, but only after surgeons had removed a kidney that was damaged by Warren when he drove a knife into the man's back.

The detectives were awaiting news of the car that Warren had stolen from the service station after killing the innocent driver. The dead man at the service station on the M5 had been strangled to death with a scarf which was left at the scene. The rest of the women's clothes found there, were confirmed to have been used by Craig Warren.

The identity of the victim revealed that he was Terence Wright, 34 years old, married with two children. He was an I.T. technician from Manchester and was on his way home, having just attended a conference in Bristol, when he was attacked while stopping for a short break.

Good news was that Peter Sherman was well enough to be released from care, and would be going home today to stay at his father's place until he was fully recovered.

Detectives Miller and Montgomery had just received another tip off from their snout. He had heard about a fence that was shifting stuff, which was reported as being similar to the items listed as stolen, as advised by the families of the knife victims.

They grabbed their coats and were off on the trail.

PC Walker and PC Davis were in the office with DCI Williams and DS Hayes giving their report on the Markham stakeout. They had confirmed the identities of the three men; Jeff Markham, Robert Morgan and the third man was Mark Wainright.

Markham as they all knew is a plasterer by trade, and sells drugs in the nightclub.

He rents an apartment on the Gloucester road.

Davis began;

'Morgan owns a garden centre on the Shurdington road, employing eight staff. He also runs his landscape gardening business from there, which employs four staff. He owns the luxurious property in Down Hatherley where Markham was followed to.

The third man we now know is Mark Wainright, he co-owns a small precision engineering company in Tewkesbury which makes parts for the car industry, and also water treatment parts for export. They employ seven staff at the unit . . .

Oh, and none of our guys has any form guv,' said Davis, 'we checked, and all three are squeaky clean according to our records.

We managed to get Wainright's name and workplace from a helpful neighbour, after tailing him home.

Apparently he only rents the property.

We also visited the engineering workshop posing as reps' so we could see what they do.

Also, I hope you don't mind guv, but we got the lab to test the bag of snort, uh . . . sorry cocaine, that Rory purchased from Markham. It was sixty percent coke, forty percent baking powder.'

'Now that's good work lads' said Hayes. 'Okay, I want you to stick with Markham for now, meanwhile I'll have someone take a look at his two high powered mates to see how they tie into this little love triangle!'

Walker and Davis left the office pleased with their little pat on the back.

'Intriguing' said Dicky, 'two business toffs entertaining a common workman till the early hours. They could be putting up the money for the drugs, and getting the plaster boy to distribute them.'

'Sounds like it.' said Hayes.

'Why don't we let Tim and Mac have a dig around to see what they come up with on these two jokers?' Dicky said, 'there isn't a lot more they can do on the Warren case now, so let them loose on this. Besides, I think Mac has a mate in the drug squad who will want in on the action, especially if these are new faces on the scene, he will want to nip them in the bud!'

'Yeah why not,' said Hayes. 'I'll go and see them now and they can get the info from Walker and Davis before they go back out.'

Hayes went off to see the two, who were in the incident room drinking coffee.

Dicky's phone rang, it was D.I. Bert Saunders at Worcester police HQ. 'Dick? Its Bert at Worcester, how are you this morning?'

'Hey Bert, I'm fine, and thanks again for your help last night at the services job, I appreciate any help I can get catching this Warren guy. He's a slippery bastard Bert and I need to get him under lock and key ASAP!'

'Yeah I know that Dick, that's why I called.

A squad car has just called in moments ago, they have eyes on the stolen BMW. It was located a couple of hours ago, in the car park of the Travel Lodge at the Sandbach service area just outside Manchester. They called us here because the theft originated from here. I thought you might want to call Manchester HQ and speak first hand to the Chief up there.'

'That's good news mate, I'll call them immediately, and thanks again I owe you a drink sometime, cheers Bert.'

Dicky was straight on the phone to Manchester and filled in the detail of the case to Chief Superintendant Brian Lawrence.

He assured Dicky that they were on the scene and would apprehend Warren if he was in the vicinity. An armed unit was about to move in at the location, and he would let Dicky know the minute they had him in custody.

FORTY.

It was three hours before Chief Superintendant Brian Lawrence called Dicky, to say that "his boys", had him in custody.

He told the story of the takedown like it was a precision SAS job. Then he informed the DCI, that Warren would be transferred over to Cheltenham custody for questioning the following morning, as long as the appropriate "prisoner transfer" paperwork was completed and correct to allow the transfer to take place.

'An operation such as this should be carried out in the correct procedural manner' he said.

When Dicky came off the telephone he was livid.

'That jumped up fucking pen pusher!' he said to Det. Hayes. 'Next thing, he'll be giving a press statement saying how "HIS" fucking boys caught the Cheltenham serial killer!.. Fucking knob head.'

'Yeah, it just shows how a bit of power can go to your head, eh Dick?' said the DS. 'Anyway, the main thing is we will have him here tomorrow.'

'You're right of course Alan, and all I can say is, I'm glad that bastard is caught. He certainly gave us the runaround. Now we can give the little shit a taste of our Gloucestershire prison hospitality.'

They both walked into the incident room where most of the team were awaiting developments on the case.

When DCI Williams gave out the news that Craig Warren was in custody, a great cheer went up in the room.

'Where and how did they get him guv, did he put up a fight?' asked DC Simmons.

'Well' said Dicky, 'Warren had stopped at a travel lodge up in the Manchester area, and just booked a room for the night. The car was spotted by a local squad car that had the details on the stolen Beemer. They called in the backup, and as there was only one door to the room, the Officer in Charge got a pass key-card from the manager, and they let themselves in.

Apparently Warren was asleep when they entered and he never resisted arrest. He went along quietly . . .

Now that's the no-bullshit version, but the OIC might tell it differently when he speaks to the press.' he said, glancing and smiling at DS Hayes.

'We will have the pleasure of Warren's company sometime tomorrow morning.'

There were a few in the room who punched the air and said 'Yesssss.' Others seemed to collapse in their chairs, as if feeling the relief of a heavy weight being lifted from their shoulders.

'Okay listen up people . . . I just want to say thanks to you all, I know some of the guys are not here at the moment, I will speak to them later. The strain of this case has taken its toll on every one of us, and I appreciate your determination to get on with it, but it proves that even with very little evidence to go on, we can still take down someone as illusive as Craig Warren. Good work. Drinks are on me after work tonight at the usual place.'

A round of hand clapping followed.

'So, Just a couple more things . . . overtime will now cease unless specifically granted by myself.'

There was a moaning sound from most in the room; they had had a free hand of working any hours required during this case, now it had to stop.

'Come on you sad buggers get a life! Spend some time with your wives, girlfriends, boyfriends etc,' said Dicky. 'Also, most of you already have cases to continue with, those of you who don't, I'm sure we can find you something.

While I am on that subject, Tim, Mac, I have a little task for you two. My office in ten minutes . . .

Alright then, let's get back to some normality around here shall we . . . oh one more thing, WPC Carter . . . ? My office now!'

WPC Elaine Carter turned as white as a ghost, and nearly collapsed at the sound of her name being called out in front of all the others in the room.

'Uh, Yes sir' she answered coyly.

There were a few 'oohs' and 'aahs' in the room, as she followed hesitantly behind DCI Williams into his office.

'Come in, shut the door and sit down!' he said to her abruptly.

She obeyed the command quickly, and then she sat shaking in the chair opposite the Detective Chief Inspector.

'How long have you been in the force now Carter?' he asked sternly.

'Uh . . . just about two year's sir.'

'And do you want to continue to be in the force Carter?'

'Yes, of course sir!'

'Doing what you are doing Carter?'

'I . . . I'm not sure what you mean sir, what have I done?'

'You haven't done anything Carter, I am just asking if you want to continue being a WPC?'

'Well . . . I guess so sir, yes.'

'You guess so, so you wouldn't be interested in becoming a detective in the CID then?'

She was so taken aback, she couldn't speak properly.

'I . . . but . . . what . . . why . . . I mean wow, yes sir I would like that very much sir!'

'Then you better learn to speak properly Carter, we can't have you blabbering like that around the office now can we?'

She sat upright in her chair as though it would help her to speak properly.

'Yes sir, or do I mean no sir?' she said.

They both burst out laughing at the same time.

'Okay Elaine I'm sorry, I couldn't help teasing you there. My colleagues and I have been most impressed with your work during your temporary transfer. Your assistance in the Warren case was commendable, and I would like to recommend that you are released from uniform to join our team in the CID . . . if you want to that is?'

'That's a definite yes from me sir, thank you.'

'Alright then, I'll put forward a formal request to the Chief Constable, asking for your permanent transfer ASAP. I am sure there will be no objections to the request. For now, I have to release you back to your "exciting job" on the beat until the Chief has given his approval of the transfer. As soon as I have that, I will contact HR and get them to prioritise the move . . .

Well Elaine, thank you for your help and I'll see you soon okay.'

She thanked the DCI and left the room with her head in the clouds.

Tim and Mac were outside the door waiting for the WPC to come out. They both gave her a high five as she passed by, they knew of the pending move already, because DS Hayes had taken a consensus of opinions from the team, regarding WPC Carter making the move to CID, it had been favorable on all counts.

Dicky called Alan Hayes, Tim and Mac into his office, he nodded to Hayes to speak.

'Right lads, you're going to enjoy this one!' he said. 'We want you to investigate a Mr Robert Morgan and a Mr Mark Wainright. Both of whom we believe to be involved in a drugs organization, along with our friend Mr Jeff Markham.

Dig up what you can on them and let me and the guv know what you find. Have a chat with PC. Davis and PC. Walker, they have been observing Markham.

Mainly we want to know how the three are linked.'

They were both happy to oblige on this one, especially if it split the gang from the "Westchester Arms" apart.

FORTY ONE.

10:30 am Saturday, the security van with Craig Warren in it arrived at Cheltenham Police station. The driver was directed to the rear of the building, where the book in desk and the holding cells were. Four uniformed officers came out to greet Warren who was handcuffed to a security officer in the back of the prisoner transfer vehicle.

They formed a gauntlet from the van to the gated entrance of the building, taking no chances with the dangerous subject. Once inside at the desk, paperwork was signed and exchanged.

Warren's personal belongings, which only consisted of a watch, some loose change, a belt and some keys; were bagged up and stowed away.

The prisoner was handed over to the custody sergeant, who read out the charges against him and asked if he understood them.

His reply was a solemn 'Yes.'

Two minutes later, the desk sergeant had him locked up in a cell.

Once the formalities were over he picked up the telephone and called DCI Williams on his home phone number.

He had requested that he be contacted at home as soon as Warren was secured in a cell.

Dicky called Alan Hayes and arranged to meet him at the station, and it was around midday when they both arrived to conduct the first interview with Craig Warren.

They sat in the office reviewing the evidence against Warren, making sure of the accusations they were to put to him shortly.

At 1:15 pm, Warren was led into interview room number one. He was directed to a chair where he sat with his handcuffed hands in his lap. The uniformed officer stepped back to the door. Minutes later the two detectives entered and sat directly opposite across the table from Warren.

After putting a new tape in the recorder and switched it to "record", DCI Williams did the formal introductions and asked the accused to state his name and date of birth for the record on the tape machine.

The prisoner complied with the request.

The DCI then read him his rights again, and informed him that he was entitled to representation if he desired. He declined the offer.

'Mr Warren, do you understand the charges against you?'

'Yep.'

'We're talking multiple murders here!' Williams said with gravity in his voice.

'Yep.'

'I can see you have no remorse . . . but please, be kind enough to tell us in your own words, why you think you can go around killing people at will!'

There was no answer.

'What crime did they commit against you?'

No answer.

'Okay then, let me tell you what we believe to have happened . . . Your sister, who was a prostitute, was murdered by a psychopathic killer who preyed on . . . shall I say certain types of women. So you decided to go out, and take out your revenge on anyone who went near, or frequented ladies of such nature. Correct . . . ?

Then you proceeded to rob them of their valuables! So, how am I doing so far? Close or not?'

The detectives waited what seemed like minutes and still no answer. Warren was sat on an incline in his chair and just kept on staring at the ceiling.

'Okay Mr. Warren, if you won't talk to us I have no option other than terminate this interview . . . We'll try again tomorrow shall we?'

No reaction, only silence.

'Right, interview terminated at 1:35 pm. Officer take him back to his cell please.'

Warren stood up and walked out silently with the custody officer, and was put back in his holding cell.

Dicky slammed his fist on the table. 'Arrogant bastard!' he said.

'Well fuck him then Alan, if he wants to tough it out that's up to him. We can go through the same tomorrow and the day after, it doesn't matter to me. He's nailed and he knows it, he's just putting on a show for us, so fuck him, we'll let him stew overnight . . . Fancy a pint?'

They went off to relax and enjoy a couple of pints at the local, after all it was the week-end!

Sunday morning they went through the same scenario.

Did he understand the charges? Yes.

Did he want representation? No.

Similar questions were asked but the silent treatment continued. So again, DCI Williams terminated the interview.

FORTY TWO.

Monday morning in the incident room everyone was fresh after their weekend off, the first for a long time.

Only Detectives Duncan Montgomery and Barney Miller had worked through, scoring a good result over the last couple of days.

Their snout had informed them of a guy who was "fencing" some stolen goods up in Birmingham, and when they checked him out. Bingo! It was Freddy, Craig Warren's contact. He was now being held in custody in Birmingham for handling stolen goods. The detectives were able to retrieve some items still in his possession, but not all, as some of them had already been sold on.

When first questioned, Freddy was asked about Craig Warren, but he denied knowing the name, which turned out to be true because Warren had used another name when he dealt with him. Only after offering to put a good word in for him if he cooperated with them, he agreed to help, and when the detectives showed Freddy a picture of Warren, he confirmed that he was the guy who had sold him the stolen goods under the name of Gary Watson.

This was another great result for the team.

The incident room was a hive of work in progress. There were cases of attempted rape, robbery with intent, car jacking from petrol stations, and more.

Detectives Clark and Mclean were gathering their evidence against the suspected drug dealers Morgan and Wainright, and they already had some interesting stuff to update their inspector with.

Earlier that morning, Dicky had sent out two uniformed officers to pick up Warren's girlfriend Sarah Hepworth and bring her into the station, he thought that Warren might crack if he saw how broke up she was.

It turned out to be a good idea, because the moment Sarah walked into the interview room where he was sitting, he broke down into tears.

Dicky and Alan were watching and listening in via the CCTV mounted in the corner of the room. Warren wasn't heard to admit anything, even though she did ask him several times if he was guilty of killing "those men", but all he kept saying to Sarah was that he was sorry and how much he loved her.

The DCI allowed Sarah twenty minutes before bringing her out of the room, they needed to get on with their questioning. This was to be the last time of trying to get a statement from him, before they had to transfer him to a high security prison pending his trial.

Alan took Sarah into another room and gave her coffee. They chatted for a while, as he tried to make sure that she didn't know the whereabouts of the hideaway that Warren had been using. Meanwhile Dicky went into the interview room with Warren and told him that they would be resuming his interview soon and that he was still entitled to have legal representation with him.

Warren surprised Dicky when he spoke, accepting the offer and asking to make a phone call.

One hour later, Warren's representative from "Glynns & Waters Associates" arrived and requested some time alone with his client. The DCI allowed them the privilege.

After forty five minutes, in which time coffee and water had been sent in on request, the barrister said that they were ready to go to interview.

Dicky and Alan both felt a change of mood as they entered and saw Warren sitting alongside his brief. His whole posture was totally different to the last two days that they had tried to get him to talk.

'Resuming the interview with Craig Warren. Monday 30th September 12:15 pm.

Present Detective Chief Inspector Williams and Detective Sergeant Hayes, Mr Craig Warren and his counsel Mr Walter Higgins.'

Det. Hayes began with the questioning.

'Craig we have enough evidence to charge you for multiple murders. We have DNA evidence, fingerprints, we have a witness, we have the surgeon's scalpel you used, and we have some of the valuables you stole from the victims.

But we want to know why?

What was your motive?

You have nothing to lose now Craig, you will be charged with the murders regardless of what you say now . . .

It's time to let go now Craig and make a full confession . . . for your family's sake, for you . . . and for your sister.'

Alan paused for effect.

'Why don't you start by telling us about your sister? We know you were very close.'

A stern look appeared on Warren's face. 'No comment.'

'You were very close to her weren't you?'

'No comment.'

'Did you kill for her?'

'No comment.'
Det. Hayes spread pictures of the victims on the table in front of Craig Warren.

'Why did you kill these men . . . what was their crime against you? Whatever you do Craig, it won't bring Carol back!'

There was no answer this time, only the tell tale pain on Craig's face as he looked over the gruesome pictures in front of him, his eyes welling with tears.

Dicky looked at Alan and indicated not to ask any more questions, he could see the grief coming out of Craig and knew he was about to pour his heart out to them, it just needed a few more minutes of patience and he would let go . . . and he did, slowly.

FORTY THREE.

With his head hanging low, he started to tell the story.

'My sister and I were twins. We grew up as close as any brother and sister could, as friends and playmates, we didn't have too many other friends, but we had each other, and it seemed, that was all that mattered.

All through school, then later and that much older and going out to work, we still spent most of our lives together.'

He looked up at the detectives; 'No it's not what you think, we were not having sex together, we were not committing *incest!* It was just a very strong bonding love that we had as brother and sister, nothing physical.

We just spent many hours together; either in her room or mine, chatting about work or some new outfits she had bought, things like that, and listening to music.

She absolutely loved "Van Morrison," she had all his albums. Her most favourite track was "Moondance", it's one of those tunes that sticks in your head, you know?

We both tried to have relationships with respective partners, but it never seemed to work out for long, our bond always seemed to bring us back together.'

He stopped talking and was weeping openly now.

'Tell us about your dad Craig,' Alan said encouraging him to continue.

'Ha . . . my dad!' he sniffed, and said with a half smile. 'He used to pick on Carol all the time. Whatever she did he found fault with her, and they would have terrible slanging matches . . . then Carol would go out, and not come home until late when she knew he had gone to bed.

Then she would come to my room to talk about dad, and I would hold her and she would cry until she fell asleep. Then it would all happen again a few days later, and the same thing went on and on and on . . . the arguments were all over nothing, until finally she decided she couldn't take it any more.

One day she came in from work and said that she was leaving home, she was going to share a flat with a work mate.

Mum and I were both devastated, and try as we may, she would not stay a moment longer with dad around.

I used to meet her after work each day, and we would talk and have coffee together, but as the weeks went by, she wanted to meet less and less, I guess she was learning to live life as she should, so I agreed and backed off until we were only meeting once a week . . .'

'It was after several months that I noticed the difference in her. She was letting herself go, you know, like not caring what she looked like, no make-up or clean clothes and that, and then she started borrowing money from me.

I did of course give her money without expecting to get it back, but I was worried what she was spending her money on . . .

It was one night after work when we were meeting for a coffee and a chat, that I decided to follow her home, wherever her home was.

So after we chatted and drank coffee, I again gave her some money because she said that her money had not gone into her bank account yet and she was broke . . . After we said goodbye, we went off in opposite directions.

I stopped further up the road, retraced my steps and quickly caught up with her, staying back in the shadows so that she didn't see me . . .

I followed her for twenty minutes, and she headed into a council estate which I knew had a reputation for drugs and other things, you know, gang crimes, car theft and stuff like that.

I was afraid not only for my sisters safety, but for myself. I held back by the side of some damaged garages as she entered a block of flats. I could see her image through the frosted glass stairwell as she climbed to the third floor, then she reappeared and walked along the outer balcony to a door about midway along.

She knocked on the door and it opened momentarily about six inches then shut. About a minute later the door opened six inches again, and she appeared to exchange something with the person behind the door, then she quickly walked back down the stairs and back out the way she had gone in.

I stepped inside the garage out of sight, and hid behind an old wardrobe that was there until I saw her pass. Then I followed her for another ten minutes to a disused railway line which had a few old carriages in a siding; she climbed aboard one and disappeared inside.

I waited, expecting her to come back out. But after five minutes or so there was no movement inside, so I crept up to the carriage and managed to climb up on a pile of railway sleepers so that I could get look through the window of the carriage, but I couldn't see her.

I started to panic.

I got down off the sleepers and then climbed up into the carriage, and there she was . . .

She was laid out on an old mattress; a strap and needle were lying on the mattress where she had dropped them after injecting the crack cocaine or whatever other shit it was into her veins.

Nearby on the floor, a small candle was still burning; alongside it was a spoon which she had used to dissolve the stuff on.

I rushed over to her and found she was barely conscious. I slapped her face thinking it would bring her around, but it didn't. I thought she was going to die.

I was about to call for an ambulance, and then thought maybe the police would come along as well, so I called for a taxi instead and took her home with me.

I managed to get her in the house and up to my room without mum and dad seeing. They were in the back room watching TV with the volume up loud because dad is a bit deaf, so they didn't even know I was home.

Anyway . . .

I made a big pot of coffee and kept encouraging her to drink it. I don't know why, I just thought that was what would bring her out of it.

It was several hours before she was able to speak to me properly.

She found it hard to confess to me, that she had lost her job. Her workmate had then kicked her out for not paying her rent, so she had to sleep rough.

She met another girl who worked as a prostitute to pay for her drug habit, and at first she just shacked up with her for somewhere to stay. Then she needed money for food and eventually drugs.

The money I gave her went on drugs, but it wasn't enough, so she started working the streets along with the other girl . . .

I couldn't believe she had stooped so low. I pleaded with her to come home and said I would help her to kick the drugs and that I would support her until she got another job.

I promised her I wouldn't let her down. I would get her back on track and everything would be like it was before she left home.

She said that was what she also wanted.

Then we hugged and talked and cried together for most of the night . . .'

There was a long silence while Warren took a sip of water from a bottle.

'What happened then Craig?' asked Dicky.

'I . . . I must have fallen asleep. When I woke up she was gone. She had taken everything I had that she could sell to pay for her habit. My wallet, watch, rings, mobile, everything.

I didn't care about that; those were just possessions that could be replaced. But she couldn't. I just wanted her back, to help make her better . . .

I searched for her for days, almost lost my job because of it.

But my boss was great, when I told him I had a serious family problem, he gave me all the time I wanted as long as I could work it off later.

But I couldn't find her . . .

I kept returning to the block of flats where I'd seen her buy that shit from, hoping she would go back there for more, but she never showed.

One time I waited there nearly all night hoping she would come . . . she didn't.

I was going out of my mind . . .

It was about two weeks after she disappeared, that the police came around to the house. They told us that they had a person in the morgue who they were fairly sure was my sister. They had found my wallet with my works identity card inside, along with a picture of me and sis taken on the pier at Weston-super-mare when we were both ten years old.

I went to the morgue to identify her; she seemed to have aged ten years, the pain of living was in the lines on her face . . . I broke down and cried like a baby . . .

But from that moment, I knew I would do something to avenge my sister. Maybe try to find the killer myself and deal him out some pain before finishing him, I didn't know what I would do to him, only that I would make him suffer more than I hope my sister had.

However it was only a few weeks later, that we found out that she had been murdered by a psycho doctor who was going around having sex with prostitutes, and then killing them afterwards. He had been apprehended by the police'

'So you thought about getting your revenge, by killing these other men purely for the reason that they associated with prostitutes?'

`I guess so.`

'Cutting them in the same way that your sister had been?' said Alan.

Craig replied in a cold controlled tone now. 'Yes.'

There was a brief pause before Dicky spoke.
'I think we'll take a short break, okay Craig?'

'Sure' he said.

FORTY FOUR.

Dicky sent coffee in for Craig and his representative, while he and Alan spoke to the Chief Constable, who had been watching via the CCTV in the recording room.

'Well Derek' said Chief Constable Barrington, 'He's certainly a cool calculated killer. The only emotion he has shown was for his dead sister. We have enough on him to put him away for a very long time, however, we should continue with the interview so that he can at least confess his crimes and maybe achieve some closure for the sake of his family.'

Back in the interview room:-

After restarting the tape recorder, Alan Hayes continued to question Warren.

'Craig, will you tell us what happened after your sister was killed, regarding yourself?'

'Why should that matter?' he testily replied.

`Just for the record, that's all,' said Dicky.

'I was ill, inconsolable, and sick to my stomach, angry.

I blamed my father for driving her away, causing her death.

I was so bad that I was sectioned, and spent a long time in an institution that treated patients who had mental disorders. I was restrained with straps and medication for some time, I'm not sure how long but no matter what they did to me, I knew that one day I would be free to avenge my sister's death.

So those long days and nights, I just played it over and over in my head what I would do when I was released, and that was what stopped me from killing myself.'

'Did you ever try to commit suicide while you were there Craig?'

'At the beginning of my stint in there yes, twice. I just couldn't see any reason to live without Carol around.

The first time, I tried to hang myself . . . then I was put in a cell with nothing but a bed and a toilet, and I was heavily sedated. They only let me out of there after I had a chat with the psychiatrist, who said that he was happy that I would not attempt to take my life again.

He was wrong! The first chance I had, I slashed my wrists with a blade from a safety razor, which I managed to steal and split open.

After that I was on 24hr surveillance, I was in a room with CCTV watching me day and night, but at least during the time I was under surveillance they couldn't beat and rape me, because of the cameras . . .

That's when I turned my mind to positive thinking and planning for when I got out, and of my duty to my sister.

The doctors were wary of me, but I played them along, and eventually convinced them that I was well, and stable enough to rejoin society.'

'So you were released, and you went back to live with your mother and father?'

'Yes . . . that was when I found out that dad had been diagnosed with full blown Alzheimer's, and all those rows he had with Carol were because he was sick, and we didn't know. I hated myself for blaming Carol's death on him, but it didn't change my mind in respect of having revenge on those who abused her.'

'At the time you returned to live in Maidenhead with your parents, did you plan to kill someone in that area?'

'Yes I did, but mum was determined to move out of the area because of the memories and upset. We also needed a smaller house.

Mum and dad only had a shitty little allowance to live on, and I had no income because I lost my job. So with the move and because of dad being ill, I delayed my plans until we moved here to Cheltenham.'

'Can you tell us about your first victim—Callum Watts?'

'I don't know their names! But I do remember the detail and the emotion from each time.

The first was the best; it was messy but so . . . ***gratifying.***

I thought to myself, that's it! I've done it; Carol can rest in peace knowing that I did it for her.

But as the weeks went by, I felt that I needed to do it again . . . I think I knew then that I would not be able to stop.

So, I decided to rent a flat so that I could go there for privacy, plus I could keep the clothes and other stuff there out of the way from mum. I didn't want her to find out about any of it, that's when I told her that I was helping homeless girls on the streets. She thought I was doing something good . . .

I used to go there when I got depressed, and I would pretend to talk to Carol, it was just a way of getting through a rough time.

I also started using dad's car so that my car wouldn't be spotted.

As far as mum was concerned, I told her that some nights of the week I needed a bigger car to transport some of the homeless young girls to a refuge, helping to get them off the streets so they didn't end up like Carol. The less she knew the better.'

'That might have been a better way to satisfy your feelings!' said Dicky.

'No . . . there was only ever one way I could do that!'

'And what about the theft of possessions from the victims, was that just a show or what?'

'It was an afterthought really, but the money from the stuff came in handy once I had pawned them off, for helping mum and dad, you know, to pay the bills and that.
So I made it part of my, what do you like to call it? "Modus Operandi".'

There was another period of silence in the room until DCI Williams spoke again.

'Craig, you know that you're charged for the murder of six men, and the attempted murder of two others. Do you wish to confess to any other criminal offences?'

'Well . . . I once nicked a Mars bar from a corner shop when I was eight years old. Does that count? Ha ha ha.'

Nobody else was laughing.

'I'll get the judge to add on another year to your sentence if I can! Oh sorry, you'll be dead won't you! Now answer the question properly!'

'No sense of humour eh, well in that case . . . no, I did what I did for my sister! And I would do it all again, and more if I had the chance!'

'Right . . . well what about the scalpel, how did you come by that?' asked DS Hayes.

'The Internet. Do you know you can buy absolutely anything on the internet? It's amazing!' Warren said excitedly.

'Yes I know; so, do you have a computer or laptop in the rented flat then?'

'Nah, I used the one in my office . . . I guess I won't be looking on E-Bay anymore though eh?'

'Probably not!' said DS Hayes. 'So where did you say the flat was?'

'Come on detective,' said Warren, 'you don't think I'm so daft as to fall into that trap, and say where my stash is, do you?'

'I wouldn't say that, no I just thought that you can't really gain anything by not telling us, that's all.'

'No I can't gain anything, but I know you want what I got.'

Warren sat in thought for a while then said. 'Well maybe, if you'll do a deal!'

'You know I'm not in a position to do a deal,' said DCI Williams.

'Then I have nothing more to say' said Craig, knowing that he had the detectives' attention..

'If I were in a position to deal, what would you be asking?'

'I've got a secret panel in the flat. I put some of the stolen items there, along with some photos of my sister. I would like the photo's back, and you can return the other things to the relatives, and we both get what we want.'

'That may not be so difficult to arrange' said the DCI, 'but I would need to consult with my superiors first.'

'It's just that I need to go there to get them, okay?' said Craig. 'I just need to go there so I can say goodbye to Carol.'

'Whoa, whoa wait a minute . . . no way. You think you're just going to be allowed to "pop out" and fetch these things after what you've done! Jesus Christ man, you've killed six people, and you'll never walk the streets again!'

Craig stared straight at the DCI, and smiling he said, 'Happy hunting then, because you'll never find the flat or the victims' valuables in a month of Sundays, without my help that is!

I do remember a nice watch from number two, the older guy; I bet his wife would be ever so grateful to get it back as a memento of her late husband!

I think I can remember the message inscribed on the back, was it . . . "To my darling George, all my love Margaret", now ain't that touching?'

The DCI was shocked at the coldness of this man before him, no compassion, and no remorse whatsoever.

'You bastard!' he said. 'We're going to terminate the interview, and then afterwards you will be taken to a holding cell until you are transferred to a high security prison, to await your trial and sentence!

It really is a pity that the death penalty cannot be given, as I would volunteer to throw the switch myself you sick fucker!'

Warren just grinned back at the DCI.

'Officer! Take him back to his cell!'

Warren still grinning just said, 'Your call detective!'

The detective called out the termination of interview time, and slammed the button to the off position on the recorder, and then he stormed out of the room.

FORTY FIVE.

The Chief Constable was not impressed with DCI Williams' outburst, but did understand how he felt. He too would flick the switch on Craig Warren given the chance. He didn't reprimand the DCI, but gave him a knowing look as they met back in his office.

'Well Derek, that was quite unbelievable, he talks about the killings like he has no soul.'

'Yeah well, he'll get what he deserves. He'll have a lot of time to think about what he did and whether it was worth it all while he's banged up.'

'Mmm . . . Now about these valuables at the flat; He knows we want the address as well as the items he left there, so I am thinking maybe we go along with it.

We let him take us there, then, at the property we simply keep him back in the police vehicle. He will be well pissed off, but tough shit, we get to go over the inside of the flat and recover the personal possessions of the victims. That might take the smile off his face!' said the Chief.

'That's your decision Chief, but I know we'll need to watch him carefully, remember he's a dangerous guy, and any chance he gets he'll be off . . . No I don't like it Sir!'

'Well I think we owe it to the victims' relatives to retrieve any items we can,' said the Chief. 'I know Margaret Pitt would be very grateful for any of her husband's belongings, especially the watch. So I will allow him the gesture, shall we say.

So Derek, will you arrange that for tomorrow morning so we can wrap this sordid mess up?'

'Yep okay, tomorrow it is if you say so Sir, I'll have the vehicles with four officers to escort him to wherever the place is.'

'Right, I'm off to give a press report now,' said the Chief. 'Jolly good work Derek, pass my thanks on to your team for their efforts, then get yourself home and enjoy the rest of the evening, I'll see you tomorrow.'

Dicky returned to the evidence room, where Alan and some of the others were waiting for him. There was a brief cheer as he entered, mainly because everyone felt the relief that the case was as good as over, just the paperwork to do now.

'Who wants a drink?' said Alan holding a bottle of scotch which he pulled out from his desk drawer.

'Well if you insist!' said Dicky, with a wry grin.

Tim and Mac had just returned to the incident room. 'Sarge!' Mac said, 'we got some news on our two big boys.'

Sergeant Hayes beckoned them into his office, Dicky followed and took a seat beside the desk as Mac began the briefing.

'Robert Morgan—as we already know, owns a garden centre and a landscape gardening business. We found out he's also a big time property developer, he has at least four large 4 storey properties in the Park area of Gloucester.

He purchases dilapidated buildings on the cheap, the bigger the better, refurbishes them, then lets them out to down and outs on benefit. It's a guaranteed income from the DHSS. This guy is a millionaire, so why get involved in drugs?

Anyway, his wife died about three years ago from cancer, and he has two kids, a son who works for a bank in London, and a daughter who dropped out of university and went trekking around the world when the mother died. We believe she is somewhere in South America at the moment.

He has a maid who comes to the house every other day for cleaning etc, and an older retired gentleman, who does odd jobs around the properties, as well as the gardens at the main home.'

'Well I think he's obviously funding the drug money, why I don't know,' said Dicky. 'And that's what we need to find out . . . What about this guy Wainright?'

Tim continued; 'Mark Wainright—he's a partner in "Pulsar Precision Engineering". It's a small company which produces some precision parts for cars built in the UK, and they also produce parts for water treatment pumping equipment, which is exported to Amsterdam.

He lives with his wife Margaret, who runs a transport company called WCS, "Wilsons Courier Service".

But, get this; it just happens to be based in the unit right next door to her husbands unit on the Tewkesbury Industrial Park.

We checked with the ferry companies, and found out that they have a regular run once a month from Harwich to Amsterdam.'

'That's interesting . . . why is it called Wilsons Courier Service?'

'Yeah . . . don't know why, we are going to dig a little deeper into the courier business, the nature of the cargo etc, and see what they carry to and fro. Maybe there's a link with the drugs here somewhere?'

'Okay Tim, Mac, good work, keep us informed.'

FORTY SIX.

Tuesday 1ˢᵗ October. 8:00 am.

DC Keith Butler and DC Sophie Smith, along with two uniform officers were ready to escort Craig Warren to the flat where they would hopefully retrieve the stolen items, plus other evidence from the murders.

SOCO, the "scenes of crimes officers", were instructed to follow the lead vehicle to the destination, and would commence their work once entry was gained to the premises.

They brought out Craig Warren from the holding cell. He had his hands behind his back with wrist restraints on.

DC Butler held out a bunch of keys that were taken from him when he was booked in at the station.

'Are the keys to the flat on here?' he said to Warren.

Craig looked at the keys and nodded confirmation. 'Yep.'

'Okay Warren, here's how it works,' said Keith. 'You will give directions to the driver of the vehicle. He'll park the vehicle as close to the entrance of the flat as possible. You stay in the car while we get out and open the door, then you can go in with us to retrieve the items, right?'

'Uh, uh . . . that don't work for me!' said Craig. 'I have a security system inside the door and it will set off within ten seconds if not shutdown. That will wake everyone in town, and I don't suppose you want an audience do you?'

'Then you just tell us the code for the system and we will disarm it!' said Sophie.

'See, now there's the problem. I can't remember the code numbers, but I know the sequence so I will have to deactivate it myself!'

Sophie looked at Keith and pulled him out of earshot to Craig. 'I don't like it, he could try to make a break for it!'

'But he's cuffed, how far would he get with those on?'

'Yeah, but he will need his hands in front to deactivate the alarm won't he? And the guv'nor told us not to take any chances with him!' she said.

'Nah, not a problem Soph, I'll take one of those new Taser guns along just in case the fucker tries it on. He won't get far after having thousands of volts shot up his arse will he!'

The Taser gun DC Butler was referring to, was a new defense weapon being tried out by the police force.

It's a gun which fires two prongs that are attached by wires, and once attached to the target, that being a human being, about 40,000 volts pass down the wires stunning and immobilizing the offender.

After the DC had gone to "sign out" a Taser and returned with it, they rejoined the officers waiting with Craig Warren.

'Right, let's get going,' said Keith.

Outside two unmarked police cars were ready and waiting. One officer, Keith and Craig went in the lead car.

One officer and Sophie followed in the other. The SOCO team joined in behind in their unmarked van.

Craig gave directions to the dingy rental, and ten minutes later they were parked outside.

The street was fairly quiet, not many people were around as it was still early morning.

They all walked up to the door of the flat.

Keith started to fumble with the keys, he found one that fitted the lock and was about to open the door when Craig said;

'Stand by for blast off . . . because that's what's going to happen the second you open that door. Believe me, the noise will deafen you and it'll wake the whole neighbourhood, and I'll stand back and let you take the flack!'

Keith thought about it for a moment, then said, 'Okay, I'm gonna switch your restraints so that your hands are in front of you, then you can operate the keypad, but I warn you, any funny business and I'll zap you with this Taser gun and shoot a million volts up your fucking arse. So don't fuck with me, we can both have what we want here, so don't play around okay?'

'Sure. No problem,' said Warren.

Keith switched the restraints from the back to the front of Craig Warren; he could now open the door and deactivate the alarm with his hands still bound.

Keith stood directly behind him with the Taser gun in his hand. 'Remember, no funny stuff!'

Craig smiled, nodded and took the keys from Keith and selected the Yale lock key.

He inserted the key into the lock, and as he turned it he looked at Keith and said cheerfully, 'Here we go then!'

At the same time as he pushed the door open Craig shouted loudly . . . '*Bang!!!*'

The sudden noise made Keith freeze momentarily, and then even before he could blink, Craig had struck him squarely on the bridge of his nose with the back of his elbow, knocking him backwards into Sophie.

Blood exploded from his broken nose. Keith fired the Taser as he fell backwards, but it shot the wires into the air.

Craig was quickly inside, door locked on the Yale and two deadbolt locks he had fitted himself, one at the top, one at the bottom of the door. He knew it would be a while before they could manage to break in through the solid door; he had time to do what he had planned.

He had fooled them easily enough; there was no alarm system on the premises, and there was no stash hidden in a secret panel.

Quickly, he made his way upstairs into the flat. He checked the fire exit door was also double bolted, and then went to the cutlery drawer in the kitchen and took out a steak knife. He went into the bedroom, picking up the photo off the dresser as he went past. He shut the door behind himself and wedged a chair under the handle.

Outside Keith was sat on the floor, stunned, with blood pouring from his nose. Sophie was already on her mobile calling for backup.

She turned and looked at Keith, 'We really fucked up here Keith, I hope we can resolve this before the guv finds out, but I have a bad feeling about it!'

'My fucking nose is broke and you're worried about the guv finding out. Warren ain`t going anywhere, he's just fucking around inside. Once the backup gets here we bust the door in, give Warren a fucking good slapping, get the gear and back to the station okay.

Now give me some more tissues for my nose!'

Backup arrived within ten minutes. Two squad cars, eight uniformed officers and "Big Bertha".

It's what they called the double handed battering ram they used to gain entry into locked properties.

Weighing in at around 25kilos, a few slams with it would shatter most door frames.

The officer who was stood ready to slam the door in said 'We're ready to go.'

Keith was standing with rolled up tissue sticking out from his nose, reset the Taser gun and said, 'Okay, but I go in first, that fucker is going to get the biggest fucking shock of his life when I get in there!'

It took four big hits to break the door in, and the uniformed officer stepped away from the broken door.

Keith stepped over the splintered wood on the floor and shouted up the stairs.

'Here comes Johnny . . . ready or not!'

'Keith . . . go careful he could have set a trap, he might even have a gun!' said Sophie.

'Don't worry babe, that fucker won't catch me out again, I'm going to whoop his arse this time.'

Sophie followed Keith up the stairs.

They entered the living room, all was quiet.

Keith called out; 'Warren, come out you arsehole, I'm gonna fry your fucking balls!'

There was no answer.

Two other officers had followed up the stairs, their steel extendable truncheons at the ready, the others were outside covering both front and back exits.

Keith, Sophie and the two officers slowly moved on through, checking the lounge and the kitchen then the bathroom, which were all clear.

The only room left was the bedroom, and the door was shut.

'He's in here then,' said Sophie cocking her thumb at the door.

'We go in on two, okay,' whispered Keith.

'Ready . . . one . . . two.' He kicked the door but it did not move due to the chair jammed tight behind it.

'Bring that fucking persuader up here on the double!' Keith yelled to the officer downstairs.

The officer came up with the battering ram and slammed it into the door two or three times before it dislodged the chair. That allowed them to kick the door wide open.

Keith stepped into the room ready to zap Warren.

He stopped abruptly.

Close behind him, Sophie gasped at the scene that lay before them.

'Oh Jesus . . . !'

They found Craig Warren laid out on the single bed.

His face was pale, white even, and his head had flopped to one side.

Eyes wide open, he was facing them as they stood in the doorway. The blood from the cut to his throat was seeping into the pillow and sheet underneath.

So much blood soaking the bed and dripping to the floor, creating a dark pool, which was already congealing like black tar in front of their eyes.

Clutched to his chest by his bloody shackled hands, was a photo of himself and Carol from their childhood days.

It was a picture taken at a funfair somewhere, Blackpool perhaps? They were smiling, having fun and eating candy floss.

They looked so happy together . . .

The steak knife was on the floor by the side of the bed where it had fallen from his grasp.

The detectives stood in silence, looking over the grim scene before them. No need to check if Craig Warren was still alive, it was obvious that he wasn't.

Nobody can lose that amount of blood, and live!

FORTY SEVEN.

Late that afternoon in the Chief Constable's office, DCI Williams and DS Hayes were sitting opposite him getting a grilling.

Although it was the Chief Constable's idea to go ahead with the trip to the hideout, it was the incompetence of the Chief Inspectors team that had bungled the operation. The press were going to have a field day with this one.

He asked DCI Williams, with a face getting redder by the second, 'How the fuck could they be so stupid, to allow a killer, who was still in handcuffs, to take advantage like that? Fucking hell Derek!'

DCI Williams spoke up in support of his team.

'Sir . . . we . . . I, appointed the two officers detailed to this job. They are both well disciplined and experienced detectives who are quite capable of a straightforward procedure such as this. Obviously Warren is . . . was, a very dangerous and conniving man, who had pre-planned his move at the premises. I can only support my team, and offer that any other one of my team, could have been duped in exactly the same way as Detectives Butler and Smith.

I will be reprimanding both officers Sir, but believe we can only learn a valuable lesson from this unfortunate trail of events.'

He was of course having a bit of a dig at his superior, for suggesting the go ahead in the first place; and he knew it.

The Chief Constable had calmed down now, and came back with, 'Yes you're right Derek, I'm sorry . . . but what the fuck do I tell the press?'

'I'm afraid I will have to leave that one with you Sir' he replied, glad that he didn't have that to contend with as well.

'Okay Derek, Alan . . . that will be all. I'll see you later.'

He stood as if to escort them out of the office.

They both went out then straight into DCI Williams' office and shut the door.

'I ought to roast those two fuckers!' he said to Alan.

'Stupid, incompetent, unprofessional, fucking brain dead wankers! All that work to catch him and they wasted it all in one move, fucking great!' he continued to rant.

'Whoa . . . Hey Dick!' save it for them eh! They do deserve a bloody good bollocking for that job, it was a total fuckup and it was their fault. I do admire you for standing up to the Chief Constable for them, but they need to know that, so when I send them in, let them have some of the flak they deserve . . . okay?'

'Okay mate, sorry, I didn't mean to take it out on you.'

Alan nodded and left the office.

He went into the very quiet incident room and instructed detectives Butler and Smith to go into the Inspectors office, "the lions den".

The roars were heard, coming through the walls of the office for the next ten minutes while the DCI berated them. Then two very red faced officers, one of them with two black eyes and a broken nose, came out looking deservedly embarrassed from their dressing down.

They both sat at their desks, heads down. Nobody in the room said a word.

DCI Williams came into the incident room about half hour later.

'Butler, Smith, I want all the evidence and information in this room appertaining to the Warren case, collected boxed and taken out of here to the records department. Also I want you to itemize everything that is going to be stored, and written up in a collated report. It will be on my desk by no later than 9am tomorrow morning, along with your written report of the incident. Got it?'

They both replied in unison, 'Got it guv.'

'Good, get on with it,' said DCI Williams turning his attention to DS Hayes, 'So where are we with the drug dealer case Alan?'

'I'll get Tim and Mac to come and update you guv, I think they are out of the building at the moment.' said Hayes.

'Okay Al;

The rest of you, lets crack on with the other cases, I want an update of all outstanding work by the morning, so get your reports ready for me by then.'

Tim and Mac had been checking out the Garden centre owned by Bob Morgan on the Shurdington road, and had just returned to the station as DS Hayes was asking their whereabouts.

Alan, Tim and Mac entered Dickys' office to bring him up to speed with the drug dealers.

'What we got Tim?' said Dicky.

Tim began, 'We just came back from the garden centre guv; we managed a sneak around in the office. Mac kept the office clerk busy while I had a quick look through the filing cabinet.

At first everything looked above board, tidy well kept files, but then I found a set of invoice papers from Amsterdam.

I only had a few minutes to scan through them, but they were not like all the other invoices.

The usual information on the invoice would show, the brand, what it is, how much of it in Kilograms, delivery dates etc, in other words, everything about the items concerned.

Now, with the invoices from Amsterdam, there is not so much information except a date and weight, and on all of them it was the same, 6000kgs. That's 6 metric tonnes. So the deliveries come in once a month, usually on the last Friday of the month, and the description given is 6 pallets of "Standard Compost".'

'So are you thinking the drugs are coming in from Amsterdam in the compost?' asked Alan.

'It's a fair chance that it could be' said Tim.

'Perhaps it is just "Standard Compost" from Amsterdam.' said Dicky.

'Could be' said Tim, 'but why import it from Amsterdam, when they are also having "Standard Compost" imported from Ireland? In fact the majority of the garden centre imports were from Ireland. There were some specialized items like porcelain pots from Spain, and shrubs from local growers amongst the invoices, but when I saw the Amsterdam papers, I cross checked with the normal files for compost, that's how I spotted it.'

Dicky sat back in his chair rubbing his chin in contemplation.

'So . . . let's put this together; let's assume the drugs come in from Amsterdam at the end of the month, possibly packaged inside the compost bags.

A metric tonne would be a whole pallet, so if the drugs were packed in the centre of the stack, the customs dogs may have a job distinguishing the smell of the drugs from the compost.

The delivery comes into the garden centre, is unpacked and the dope removed.'

Mac jumped in with his thoughts, 'That means that there could be another person involved with the gang working at the garden centre.'

'Possibly' said Dicky, 'then, let's say that it gets taken to Robert Morgan's house, where they cut and mix the stuff before distribution.

Markham and Wainright pop around for a drink and a chat, and go home with a take away bag of dope!'

'Sounds a good theory to me guys, all we need now is the evidence to back it up with!' said Alan.

'Well then,' said Dicky, 'let's sleep on it, and in the morning we set out a plan to snare these dope sellers. At some point we will have to involve the drugs squad and our colleagues in Amsterdam . . .

We have a bit of time on our side if they stick to their end of month schedule.

The next shipment should be in about 4 weeks, which gives us plenty of time to put things into place.

Okay guys, who fancies a beer?'

FORTY EIGHT.

During the following week, plans were prepared and put in place ready to catch the drug dealers in action.

Operations were broken down into small stages, the drug squad demanded full control of the situation, with backup from the investigating officers.

By backtracking the courier company "WCS" based in Tewkesbury, who brought in the deliveries to the garden centre from Amsterdam, Cheltenham constabulary drug squad, in conjunction with the Dutch drug enforcers, were able to locate the warehouse where the gear came from.

It was owned by a known drug cartel which has been under investigation for the last 9 months. The Dutch team was just about ready to take them down when they heard from Cheltenham, so the information from this side of the water was welcomed, and they were more than happy to integrate the operations hoping to take out more of the gang links on this side of the water.

The Dutch police would be monitoring things on their side, and would be in constant communication with Cheltenham. They would wait until the load for the garden centre was on its way, then move in on the warehouse, make arrests and close them down.

Customs and Excise were put in the picture; their role would be to impound the lorry once it was UK side. The pallet, or pallets bound for Gloucester, would be checked to see if the drugs were concealed in the compost. If the check was positive, the driver would be arrested and charged. A tracking device would be put into one of the packages, and then a replacement driver would take over, and continue the delivery to the garden centre to drop off the load as expected.

When the tracking device indicated that the load from the garden centre was on the move, the Drug squad assisted by detectives from Cheltenham would be ready to follow and move in.

It was still assumed that the drugs would go to Robert Morgan's house in Down Hatherley, for cutting and distribution.

It had not been confirmed, but the indications were that there was a workshop at the back of the house, which was being used for this purpose. It was a risk they were willing to take, especially if the packages were delivered there.

A team would be situated near to Morgan's house ready to move in. Similar teams would be ready at Markham's apartment and Wainright's house, also at the Engineering workshop and Courier units in Tewkesbury.

Everything was in place, so all they had to do now was await the deadline.

DCI Williams was hoping for a good result on this one, it might put him and his team back in the Chief Constable's good books, even though the operation was to be controlled by the drug squad, closely followed by the customs and excise crew, the Detectives were merely adding a bit of clout to the takedown.

Meanwhile, the Chief Inspector had tails put on the three targets, Markham, Morgan and Wainright.

FORTY NINE.

It was the day of Craig Warren's funeral, twelve days since he had taken his own life.

DCI Williams was not looking forward to the ceremony that he and DS Hayes were compelled to attend. It was supposed to be a small gathering of Warren's friends and family only, but it was expected to be a chance for the press and other people to vent their anger. The police would need to be present to avoid confrontation; the family should have the right to mourn their son regardless of his crimes.

The detectives arrived at 10:30 am, awaiting the arrival of the small group of mourners.

The service was scheduled for 11:00 am at the Cheltenham Crematorium, and trouble was expected.

Already there were people milling around outside the entrance to the sacred grounds. Officers were blocking the entrance and had orders only to allow the funeral procession of the Hearse and three cars through.

The family arrangements had been restricted due to the possibility of protestors at the crematorium, so only thirteen people in all were to attend.

Including the two detectives they were; the mother and father of Craig Warren, Sarah, the fiancée of the deceased, Kev & Lynn, Dave & Karen, Spike & Angie, Danny & Maggie.

By 10:45 am there was a big crowd awaiting the arrival of the Hearse that was carrying the corpse of the killer. Amongst the crowd were relatives of the deceased victims, along with other protestors of sorts, and of course the media.

TV, press reporters and their equipment, formed a line like a gauntlet for the procession to pass through. It would guarantee them the best coverage for their voyeuristic public.

They had had more than a week of headlining the stories and reports regarding the murders, now they would have a last chance to report the demise of the serial killer.

At 10:50 am, the Hearse followed by the three cars turned slowly into the end of the road leading up to the crematorium entrance gates.

The crowd of protestors and photographers enveloped the cars; people were banging on the bodywork of the vehicles with banners and shouting abuse.

The photographers' cameras were flashing at the windows of the cars, battling against each other to get the best shot. The police moved forward to hold back the angry crowd and allow the procession of cars get through the gates.

The Hearse pulled up outside close to the buildings entrance doors. The family and friends got out of the cars and filed quickly into the sacred house.

The coffin was extracted from the rear of the Hearst, to a chorus of loud booing and jeering from the unruly angry crowd at the gates.

It was a very short service, at which not one of the people present stood to say any words about Craig Warren.

The mother wept, as did Sarah. The father just gazed around himself as though he was on an outing to see the architecture. The friends all just sat close together, silently bewildered by the whole thing.

The church echoed to the words spoken by the Vicar, as he told of the journey the deceased would be taking.

The Holy words of the preacher were no different for a killer or a saint; to people with religious beliefs, anyone who enters the house of God deserves the same respectful ending, and a promise of eternal life in a room prepared by the Lord himself.

The crowd outside appeared to totally disagree with this philosophy, and given the chance they would have smashed up the coffin, and mutilated the corpse right there and then.

In less than fifteen minutes it was all over. The coffin disappeared behind a curtain, while the music of a hymn played softly, yet ghostly, through the speakers mounted in the cold dark arches that formed the side walls of the building.

The small congregation rose and exited the echoing room to more loud abuse outside.

The two detectives escorted the friends and family to the cars, and they were driven away through the maddening crowd.

There was no tea and sandwiches prepared for afterwards, but the group was offered to come in for a drink when they returned to the Warren household.

They all felt obliged, besides, Sarah was their best friend and she hadn't committed any crime, so they politely accepted the offer.

Arthur Warren was led indoors to his chair by the window, and promptly fell asleep.

Silvia Warren and Sarah fetched the drinks, some coffee for the women and cans of beer for the men. The women sat and the men stood, all in silence for a long while, then Danny spoke as he raised his can of beer.

'Here's to Craig!' he said, 'No matter what he did or what they say about him, he was our mate, and that's how I will always remember him!'

They were all in agreement, he was their friend and that's the only Craig they knew, not the serial killer.

They raised their drinks to him.

Sarah was brokenhearted, and being comforted by this strong woman, who was Craig's mother.

'If only he could have told us how he felt!' said Sarah looking at the others, 'Maybe we could have helped him, and perhaps he wouldn't be dead now . . . if only.'

FIFTY.

During the weeks of waiting before the next delivery, the drugs gang was under constant close observation.

Markham had made four trips to Morgan's house, along with his sports hold-all, so he was taking gear away in weekly doses. He was still observed selling the coke at the club on Thursday nights, and he was possibly selling some inside "The Westchester", but the observers never entered the pub in case they were spotted by Markham. They were told by the guv'nor to give him some rope, they would hang him later.

Wainright drove his BMW to work at the Tewkesbury engineering workshop each day, only staying for a short period before returning home. He only visited Morgan twice in the month, both times he took a hold-all from his car into the outhouse, returning it to the boot of his car when he left.

Morgan himself, took two trips to the garden centre, but otherwise rarely stepped outside of his own gated property.

He was seen most days, to spend a lot of time in the outhouse alongside the house, sometimes accompanied by his odd job gardener guy.

Delivery week.

Thursday at 10:00 am. The courier lorry was being loaded with pallets at the warehouse just outside of Amsterdam. The Dutch authorities were about 100 metres from the loading bay, watching through high power surveillance cameras as the lorry was loaded.

Two hours later, with its load secure, it moved out and headed for the Dutch ferry port of Ijmuiden, at The Hook of Holland, about an hours drive from the warehouse.

An unmarked police car followed at a distance to confirm the boarding of the lorry on to the ferry, heading for Harwich England.

Once this was confirmed and the ferry on its way out to sea, Harwich C&E officers were informed, who in turn told Cheltenham CID that the load was incoming.

Meanwhile, the Dutch drug enforcers had moved in at speed on the warehouse in Holland, trapping twelve workers and three big drug barons on the premises.

The warehouse contained pallets of the "Standard Compost" which was a genuine product, but used merely for cover by the drug dealers.

Cocaine in 2 kilo bags was being hidden in the centre of pallets ready to be shipped out.

The team found 250 kilos of cocaine in 2 kilo bags about to be smuggled out with the compost bags, putting 10 kilos per pallet, at a street value of around 60,000GBP per kilo.

They realized that this factory was just a middle man operation, however, it was a good result and would send out a message to those higher up in the chain.

Stage one was complete, and the C&E officers were ready and waiting at the ferry port in Harwich England for the ferry to arrive with the precious cargo.

With a 2:00 pm departure time and approx 5 hours sailing, it was due in at 7:00 pm.

The ferry was on time, docking at 7:03 pm. The lorry rolled off the ferry at 7:30 pm and was directed into an inspection bay by customs officers.

The driver was questioned about his load as the officers went to work on the cargo to check that the drugs were onboard.

The driver, Frank Gray who was British nationality, said that he did the run once a month, and was told not to ask any questions about the cargo. As far as he was concerned, it was just pallets of compost that he had to deliver with a promise of a bonus in his pay packet.

His said that his employer was Margaret Wilson, who owned the small courier service "WCS", the detectives knew her to be Margaret Wainright.

The officers already had this information which had been uncovered by Detectives Clark and Mclean, they could only assume that it was registered in another surname for tax purposes, it may even be her maiden name, however they would find out later.

The driver's job was to deliver engineered water treatment parts from Wainright's "Pulsar Precision

Engineering" company in Tewkesbury, to Holland on the out trip, and then pick up the pallets of compost for Morgan's garden centre for the return journey.

Very convenient for the drug smugglers.

According to his delivery schedule, he had just the one drop off next morning which was at the Shurdington garden centre in Gloucester, the vehicle would then be returned to the Tewkesbury unit.

Gray the driver, was shitting it because he knew what he was carrying was probably illegal, but didn't really have a clue of the money involved.

He was going to be charged and held in custody until the operation was complete.

The search of the six pallets confirmed that one of them was concealing 5 bags, approx 10kilos of cocaine.

Customs had noticed that the pallet with the contraband had a slightly different colour coded label on the outside of the packaging, probably to identify it from the others when it was unloaded.

A tracking transmitter was put inside one of the drugs packages, then the packages were repacked amongst the compost on the pallet as before.

The new driver was to be an undercover customs man; his job was to complete the delivery as scheduled by the "WCS" boss.

The "WCS" driver Frank Gray, said that his instructions were to drive to the Tewkesbury unit leased by Margaret Wilson (Wainright). The lorry would then park up overnight in their warehouse, and he would return to make his delivery the following morning.

This was the first problem the customs men had, because their undercover driver would be seen and obviously recognized as not being one of Margaret Wainright's staff. This would alert someone, and then the whole operation would go tits up.

It was time to change the plan; they needed the help of Frank Gray the "WCS" driver otherwise this could all go wrong.

They brought him back in the office and made him an offer he couldn't refuse.

They guaranteed he would get off light, without prosecution or loss of his license, only if he cooperated with them.

To their relief he accepted.

So stage two was complete, and the real "WCS" driver set off from the ferry port on the 3 hour journey heading towards Tewkesbury with the goods, followed by two unmarked patrol cars providing an escort for the lorry.

He was told to follow the usual procedure, of parking the lorry in the warehouse unit overnight, then return and complete the delivery the following morning. The only difference being, he would be spending the night in a cell, and then escorted back to work the next morning at 10:00 am.

He always started at this time when he had come back from a run to Holland, because he was allowed a minimum of an 8hour break.

The journey was complete at around midnight. The driver unlocked the small entry door set within the main door, with his own set of keys, and entered inside. A minute later, the large roller door to the unit went up to the full extent of the opening. The driver reversed the lorry inside, parking it face forward ready to drive out the next morning.

He closed the roller door down, came out of the small door and relocked it. Then he walked around the corner out of sight to an unmarked police car, which was waiting there to take him into custody for the night.

Surveillance on the lorry would be difficult, simply because it would be out of sight in the locked-up warehouse, but a police surveillance car would be parked up outside throughout the night.

A fresh surveillance team in an unmarked squad car, parked up in position opposite the unit doors, ready for the long night's stint.

FIFTY ONE.

Friday morning 8:00 am.

Four officers, who were part of the "take down" group, relieved the guys who had sat all night in an unmarked squad car, watching the unit and the tracking receiver signal.

This group along with four others, who were already on site, was going to enter the warehouse and the engineering premises as soon as the lorry had left with the delivery. All employees would be transported to the station and held over until the operation was complete, and both units would be searched for any evidence of drugs.

Another unmarked squad car would carry the receiver and follow the lorry when it delivered the drugs.

The officers' surveillance log read:-

7:30am, Wainright's "Pulsar Precision Engineering Company" unit, was opened up by a middle aged man; he appeared to put all the lights and heating on.

7:50am, the other workers arrived and by 8:00am had started work.

At 8:30am, a Mercedes coupé pulled up outside the engineering unit.
Mark Wainright stepped out of the car driven by his wife.
Carrying a brief case, he entered his unit, speaking to the workers as he walked through to the office at the rear.
Margaret Wainright also got out carrying a briefcase. She locked her car, and then unlocked the entrance door that was in the middle of the main roller door, then stepped inside closing it behind her.

Officers on duty could see the fluorescent lights go on inside. They assumed this to be the usual morning routine.

At 8:45am, two more men arrived by car. They parked in the staff car park at the side, and entered the "WCS" unit.

At 9:00am the officers could hear movement inside the "WCS" unit. After checking with control to find out whether to move in or not, they were told to hold position, but allow one officer to try and get a closer look to see what was going on.

One officer investigated movement in building. One of the men inside was operating a diesel forklift, he was moving empty pallets around, and loading them onto a trailer bed of a lorry. He could also see Mrs. Wainright in her office at the rear, talking to the other employee.

On return to the unmarked surveillance car, the officer radioed back to control informing them that all looked quite normal.

Control advised officers to hold position, movement of the cocaine would be indicated by the scanner, and that wouldn't be until the driver came in at 10:00am to deliver the load to the garden centre.

At 09:45 am, the driver was dropped off around the corner from the unit by an officer in another unmarked car, after his night in the cells. He knew he had to cooperate with the police, or be tried and prosecuted for his involvement in the handling of illegally imported drugs.

He had no choice but to play his part in the takedown of the drug dealing gang.

As he was about to enter the unit, Mrs. Wainright came out of the small door and spoke casually to him..

'Morning Frank . . . good trip I hope?'

'Yes, fine Mrs Wilson.'

'Good, well when you've delivered to the garden centre, can you come back here and help Roy and

Martin tidy up, and then return some of those pallets back to the pallet store. I need to pop home for a while, I'll be back around lunchtime okay?'

'Sure thing Ma'am, no problem,' he replied.

The surveillance guys called control again, after hearing what Mrs. Wainright had said. Again they were told to hold position because there was another team watching the Wainright house ready to move in for the search.

10:00 am, and the big roller door started to lift up, one of the two workers was at the control box operating it.

The cooperative driver was in the lorry ready to drive out, and as the door reached its limit and stopped, the driver started up the lorry and drove out.

The officers were informed by the tracking receiver in their car, that the pallet on the lorry was on the move, which is what they expected. So far so good.

The tracking car which had two officers, Detectives Mclean and Clark in, followed the lorry heading towards the garden centre.

Officers from two other cars at the industrial park moved in on the two units, four men into each. At the same time, two vans arrived, it was the transport for the workers to be taken down to the nick.

The people were escorted aboard the vehicles, and the search of the units commenced.

Mark Wainright was not there!

The middle age guy who had opened up the unit, who was the other partner, said that Wainright had come in to collect something from the office; he then left the building through the emergency exit at the rear of the workshop.

An officer called control and informed DS Hayes, who was the controlling officer down at headquarters, that Mark Wainright had disappeared via the emergency exit of the engineering unit.

The team stationed at the Wainrights' house reported that Mark Wainright left his house 30 minutes earlier than his wife. He was driving his BMW and she was driving her Mercedes coupé. Neither had returned since.

The team were unsure what the Wainrights' were up to. They had arrived at the unit together in the wife's car, and then he sneaks out of the back door while she leaves by the front.

The co-owner of the engineering company said that Mark Wainright was a sleeping partner, and very rarely attended the unit unless there was a need to, although this last couple of weeks he had been to the unit nearly every day but never stayed long.

He would come in, do a bit of paperwork, have a cup of tea and a chat with the guys, then leave. It seemed like it was becoming a daily ritual.

The other mystery was that Margaret Wainright said she had to go home for something, but as yet she had not arrived!

Twenty minutes later, the lorry pulled into the garden centre and parked outside the warehouse store at the rear of the centre.

It was a further ten minutes or so, before a forklift driver arrived to unload the pallets into the store. The transmitter had worked and indicated a GPS reference of the goods on the pallet.

Another car with two drug squad officers, pulled alongside the car of detectives Mclean and Clark, waiting in the car park for further movement. They were expecting someone to remove the drugs from the pallet and deliver them to Robert Morgan's house. They did not know who would do this, or when this would take place, but believed it was too valuable to be left too long.

It might all go down after closing time when the other workers had left, that could mean it was someone who was in charge of the keys to lock up. Once the gear was moved to Morgan's premises, the officers would move in and the final takedown would happen.

The driver took the empty lorry back to the Tewkesbury unit, accompanied by a patrol car which would take him back into custody. Once there he would be required to make a full statement, which would eventually be evidence used against the drug dealers.

It was now past midday, and still no movement indicated by the sensor even though it was still active.

The two cars with all the officers sat inside, were beginning to stand out in the fairly empty car park of the garden centre, so much so that one of the employees on his lunch break approached one of the cars and asked if he could help.

One of the officers from the drug squad dealt with him. He explained that they had been given a tip off that there was going to be an attempted robbery, so they were staking it out until they heard otherwise from control.

The employee was taken by surprise and very concerned, he said he would need to call his boss Mr. Morgan and let him know.

The officer told the man that on no account should he do that, as it might jeopardize any chance of an arrest, so just carry on as normal and they would inform him if something was about to start.

He also asked the man to be vigilant and report to them personally, any unusual behaviour by customers.

The employee was keen to help, and rather excited that he may be part of an arrest, and the officer was happy that he had easily got away with the bullshit story.

FIFTY TWO.

By late afternoon, the team in the control room were getting worried. There had been no movement of the drugs according to the tracking device.

The team watching at Morgan's house reported nothing unusual there, Morgan had been in and out of the house a couple of times, spending more time in his workshop again than in the house; Other than that, no visitors.

The team at Wainrights' place was even more concerned, because nobody had returned since leaving that morning and there was no other movement from the house.

The guys at control had to make a decision on the next course of action, the longer they waited the more chance the drug dealers had a chance of suspecting something going on. If the Wainrights were to go back to the Tewkesbury units, they would definitely know something was going down as their employees were all at the station being interviewed.

A bulletin was put out to all patrol units to be on the look out for the Wainrights, they needed to be found and detained in custody ASAP.

The word from control to the team guarding the dope, was to wait at the garden centre until closing time, which was 7:00 pm, and then they would have to move in and check the drug consignment in the store room. They would use the manager who locked up at night to gain access.

They were convinced that Morgan would not leave the drugs in the store all night, but he may come to fetch them later when all the staff have gone home.

The two officers watching Jeff Markham, reported that he had remained at work all day, no sign of movement from him, as expected.

It was a long drag waiting for the clock to reach the deadline.

Finally at 7:00 pm, the staff at the garden centre were making moves to close and lock up the store.

The helpful employee came across to the car again.

'So, what's happening?' he asked.

'We're not sure yet' said the officer, 'the best thing you can do is get on home, we will continue here, and thanks for your help.'

'I can stay on a bit later if you want me to help in any way?' said the man looking disappointed.

'No, it's best that you leave it to us, okay? and thanks again. Oh, and remember not a word to anyone, we don't want to startle the robbers do we?'

With that, the disgruntled helper nodded then went back inside the shop.

Five minutes past by before the staff filed out. The helpful worker gave them a wave as he rode past on his bicycle.

The last person to come out of the store was a woman. She had turned out the lights and was starting to lock the outer doors; one of the officers went across and showed her his identity card and told her that he and his colleagues needed to check on something in the store room.

'I'll have to call Mr Morgan first' she said; another loyal staff member.

The officer gave another bullshit story, saying that there was a possible bomb threat and that they needed to check it out immediately, and there was no time to call Mr. Morgan, they would contact him after the check.

She very reluctantly agreed as long as they promised to inform her boss.

The team informed control that they were about to check out the drugs, and to put a hold on all the teams until their position was clarified.

As long as the drugs were still safe, it would still be just a matter of waiting.

One detective took the manageress to one side away from the store, making it look like a real bomb threat.

'Shouldn't they all be wearing one of those protective suits like you see on the telly?' she asked inquisitively.

'Nah, these guys are professionals, they know what they're doing,` said DS Clark, piling on the bullshit.

The two drug officers along with DC Maclean, entered the store room and found the marked pallet containing the transmitter, it had another pallet on top of it.

'Shit, we're going to need a forklift now!' said one of the officers.

'No worries' said Mac, 'I know how to drive one, we just need the key.'

He went outside and asked the manageress where the keys to the forklifts were; again she was reluctant to tell him, but finally relented.

She was getting more suspicious of the men now, and opening her bag took out her mobile phone and began to dial Robert Morgan. DS Clark had to physically stop her by wrenching the phone from her grip. Now she knew there was something wrong, and started to become rowdy.

The detective tried to calm her down, but she continued to berate him, accusing them of trickery to gain entry to the store, she wanted to call the police.

Even after showing her his badge she continued, so he had no choice but to put a set of restraints on her and put her in the back of the car.

Meanwhile, Mac got on the electric Lansing Bagnall forklift truck and maneuvered it to pick up the top pallet. He moved it across the store out of the way, so they had access to the bottom one. Together the men moved the top bags of compost, so they could expose the drug bags in the middle.

They all stood back in horror.

There were no drugs, just a plastic bag with the transmitter and a piece of notepaper inside.

One of the drug squad officers put on a pair of rubber crime scene gloves. He picked up the bag and took out the transmitter and the note.

He opened the piece of paper and read it, 'Bollocks! We've been had.'

The note said;

'Sorry guys, better luck next time!'

FIFTY THREE.

When the garden centre team reported the findings to control, it didn't go down too well.

Inspector Max Peters who was heading the operation for the drug squad was Livid.

A big operation as this, and all could be lost. He decided that they had to make the move regardless. All the search warrants were approved and ready, the officers were in place, so he ordered all teams to move in, apprehend and search premises.

An all points bulletin was out for the Wainright's, their descriptions and car registrations, they were to be apprehended as soon as possible, it was clear that they had possession of the drugs.

Two officers arrested Jeff Markham who had just finished work, and a team searched his place of work, but came up empty handed.

Another team searched his home. They found about twenty "coke baggies" hidden in a Tupperware container under the kitchen sink behind some household cleaning items.

At the Wainright's home, the squad found the back door unlocked, so there was no need to break it down as they had expected.

Inside the house, the downstairs rooms looked like a normal household, nothing very fancy, standard run of the mill furniture and décor. Not really the type of home you would expect a drug baron to live in.

Upstairs they found no drugs in the main bedroom, but in another room they did find some weighing scales, the kind used by dealers for measuring before "bagging", they were left on top of a glass top table. Traces of either cocaine or baking powder were also visible, probably the latter. Two chairs accompanied the table, and a box of surgical gloves and paper masks like the ones used in hospitals were on the floor beside it.

It looked like they had spent cozy nights weighing and bagging coke together.

While searching the premises, it was very evident that the Wainright's had taken their clothes and belongings. All the indications were that they had done a runner!

SOCO arrived and began to do their stuff.

Meanwhile an eight man team had moved in on Morgan.

They used a plain clothed female officer to coax him out to the gate and open it, pretending that her car had broken down and that she was in need of a telephone, and use of a bathroom.

As he opened the electronic gates, the men moved in. Morgan tried to protest, but realized it was futile, as a detective waived a search warrant under his nose, and the officers were already storming in onto his property.

He would not have time to dispose of any drugs in his possession.

A search of the expensively clad house came up with nothing, but the search of the outside workshop where Morgan spent a lot of his days, revealed that he was a talented artist, and spent a lot of his time just painting still life.

There was a half finished portrait of the old gentleman gardener, who had been posing part time for Morgan in between working, it was set upon an easel at one end of the workshop.

On another easel was a painting of a `Bonsai tree` that he was also currently working on.

A perfectly manicured real Bonsai tree, was on top of a stand in front and to the left of the artist's work in progress canvass.

The whole workshop was filled with canvasses, some finished, some part complete, and some blank. There were oil paints of all colours set out in racks above a workbench, which itself was littered with jugs full of brushes, artist's pallets and a few rags with paint dabs on them.

Not discouraged, they continued a thorough search and uncovered an amount of drugs already "bagged" and ready for sale, in a metal locker where some other paint tins were stored.

There was approximately half kilo of cocaine in bags the same as Markham was selling at the club.

This was not the drug factory that they were expecting to find!

FIFTY FOUR.

In the debrief of the drug dealers' takedown operation, which was held a few days later, the result was not very impressive.

Representatives from each of the divisions, sat and discussed the results and the failures of the combined operation.

The investigation team comprised of :-

Head of drug enforcement for Holland—Chief Inspector Johann Weiss.

Lead investigator for Cheltenham CID—Detective Chief Inspector Derek Williams and Detective Sergeant Alan Hayes. Cheltenham CID.

Head of West Midlands drugs & vice squad investigations—Superintendant Graham Morton.

Lead investigator for drugs & vice squad—Detective Inspector Max Peters and assistant Detective Sergeant Barry Richards.

South East Her Majesty's Customs and Excise—Inspector Henry Gordon.

The Dutch drug enforcers were relatively happy with their results; they had broken up a factory, recovered a stash of drugs destined for distribution, and bagged several big players. A good score for them, against the prolific drug problem they have in their country.

However, for the British contingent of the operation, it had been a disaster and an embarrassment.

The key offenders had managed to elude capture.

All they had to show for all the effort, was 2 men being held for possession of approximately one and a half kilos of cocaine between them, and both Morgan and Markham had admitted possession, but that it was for their own personal use.

Both denied charges of dealing and distribution of an "A" class drug.

The evidence against the perpetrators was not very strong, even with the witnessing of selling drugs at the club, it would be dismissed because the officer had bought from Markham.

He would merely have to say that the officer was a regular customer, and the high powered barrister who Morgan had hired with his wealth, would shred the evidence to pieces, defending Morgan and Markham.

Statements from both of them only revealed that Mark and Margaret Wainright were their suppliers. They denied any other connection with them regarding distribution.

It would be difficult to prove that Mark Wainright supplied the drugs to Morgan and Markham for distribution now that he had disappeared.

In his statement, Robert Morgan also said that he had become very depressed when his wife passed away, and turned to drugs before becoming interested in art.

He hadn't realized his skill as an artist, until after drug rehabilitation, he found it to be stress relieving, and gave him the peace and tranquility he desired.

He did however, admit to faltering in his rehabilitation, and had recently started using the drug again.

When asked about Markham and Wainright visiting his home, Morgan said, that occasionally they liked a snort of coke and a game of poker, and that they also liked to see his art work when they visited.

Jeff Markham said in his statement, that he had been offered some of the drugs at a party that he and Mr Morgan had both attended, held at Mr and Mrs Wainright's house.

It was there that he was first introduced to Mr Morgan, and where he was also offered some work on properties that Morgan had purchased and was having refurbished.

The only other person held briefly, was Roy Slater, one of Margaret Wainright's workers from the unit. His fingerprints were found on some of the bags of compost which were on the pallet carrying the drugs.

He admitted to moving bags of compost that were on the pallet, but denied any knowledge of concealed drugs. He also denied knowing the whereabouts of the Wainrights.

He was later released without charges, due to lack of evidence.

The representatives came to the conclusion that the Wainrights were the main players behind this little syndicate on this side of the water. It became evident that they were the ones who imported the drugs, then cut and "bagged them, while Markham sold them on and Morgan probably financed it.

But they had now disappeared, only leaving behind fingerprints taken from both cars, which were found abandoned. Even their identities were unconfirmed, and were probably false.

Investigations found nothing on the two dealers whatsoever, not even a bank account or telephone bill. They had both used "Pay-as-you-go" mobile phones, and when the numbers were traced by using Robert Morgan's phone bill records, the two connections were dead.

Their cars, the BMW and the Mercedes coupé, were both found parked up in the Tesco car park in Tewkesbury. It appears that they had abandoned them, and made their escape in another unknown vehicle.

It was discovered later, that both cars were on a monthly lease from the same leasing firm.

Likewise the house; the Wainrights had also rented the property complete with furniture, hence the modest décor.

Obviously their intention was not to stay, but make some big money and then move on.

Mark Wainright's partnership with the engineering company, was just a means of being in touch with the haulage contract that his wife was coordinating. He had obviously made a calculated loss, and forfeited his partnership at the end.

Margaret Wainright's unit was on a short term lease, as were the Lorries and lifting equipment, again a small forfeit for the profit they were making on the dope.

During an informal end to the meeting, questions and possible theories were proposed from all sides, most of which became clear after discussion.

The only query they had which could not be answered confidently was—How the hell did the Wainrights' know the drugs contained a transmitter?

The only answer they could come up with was that there was an informer who tipped them off, and the Wainrights' had played them along all the way.

Accusations were made, that the obvious person to inform them had to be from Customs and Excise.

Henry Gordon was quick to defend his men, saying that the officers involved in the operation were honest and committed men, and he objected to his men becoming scapegoats for a cock up.

He only agreed to an internal inquiry, if all the other combined services did the same, because there was nothing to say that one of the detectives from Cheltenham or Holland were not involved. The other representatives conceded that everyone who was involved in the operation, all had full knowledge of the plan.

The conclusion was that it was very likely that the couple had fled the country, and would set up their dangerous but lucrative business elsewhere, under another name.

Authorities across Europe were informed, and would have received detailed descriptions of the Wainrights, including fingerprints.

Should they appear, they would be arrested and deported back to the UK to face charges, but the chances are that they would already have changed their identities and be no longer recognizable.

The Internal inquiries that followed from the meeting, did not uncover the informer, he is still unknown and still out there!

Robert Morgan did not let the authorities know just how pissed off he was. He had paid Mark Wainright 160 grand the week before the takedown, for financing the purchase of a larger consignment of drugs, and now to find out that the couple had done a runner really made him mad.

A double whammy as far as he was concerned!

But Morgan has friends in high places, and already the word is out on Mr Wainright, and when they find him, he's going to suffer and pay back big time.

Is this the end?

Other Books of Stephen Lawrence

"THE MAJOR"

"Ex Army officer Captain Peter Wicks, now medically discharged and living in the Cotswold's with his wife Jessie, receives a mysterious offer of employment days before his 45th birthday. Accepting the well paid offer, he finds himself embroiled in a web of espionage, blackmail, arms deals and assassinations. He later finds out that it's more difficult to break free from the organization than it was to join it.

How can he detach himself from the grip of 'The Major' and his organization, whilst he and his family are under threat? Will his friend at GCHQ help him to expose the man who poses a danger to him, his friends, his family and his marriage . . . ?"

"LUKE"

"A successful career minded young couple, Tom and Pat Dalton and their 2 children, move into an old Tudor house unaware of its previous history. Jamie their young son thinks it's the best place ever, especially because the house comes with a resident cat, lots of interesting places to explore, and a new playmate from the neighborhood called Luke.

Their teenage daughter Sarah, who has to settle into her new school adds to the stress, but it's not because of her studies.

The parents however, soon have reservations about the move to their new dwelling after some strange things begin to happen, and they begin to find out the sordid history that goes with the house . . ."